Terror on the Peninsula

TERROR ON THE PENINSULA

The Larucci Files

A Novel

By

DANA L. COY

Order this book online at www.trafford.com
or email orders@trafford.com

Most Trafford titles are also available at major online book retailers.

Author of "Flying Above the Pinnacle - Memoirs of An Alaskan Pilot"
Michelle Juett for Cover and Graphics

This is a work of fiction. All of the characters, names, incidents, organizations, and dialogue
in this novel are either the products of the author's imagination or are used fictitiously.

Printed in the United States of America.

ISBN: 978-1-4269-3472-8 (sc)
ISBN: 978-1-4269-3473-5 (hc)

Library of Congress Control Number: 2010917605

Trafford rev. 12/29/2010

 www.trafford.com

North America & international
toll-free: 1 888 232 4444 (USA & Canada)
phone: 250 383 6864 ♦ fax: 812 355 4082

Foreword

Few people know more about the distinctive features, the ever-threatening waters, and harsh terrain of the Alaskan peninsula than the pilots flying the skies above it on daily routes. Without the pilots and the services they bring to the region, the small fishing towns and villages would cease to exist. High winds and continual rain mercilessly pound the peninsula. With the scars of abandoned and overgrown airstrips and an occasional uninhabited settlement—the struggle for existence is never ending. Appearing as a mere slice of land from Dutch Harbor to King Salmon, this appendage, dividing two large bodies of water, can be extremely unforgiving. On occasion, a deserted ship, a product of a sleepy captain or shoddy equipment, can be seen stranded on the rocky shoals or beaches, its fate to be determined by the cruel seas caressing an isolated tomb. No roads run the length of this land.

Local pilots know the peculiarities of the peninsula and are well-informed of new activities or changes that may occur from day to day. These courageous and daring souls are the Alaskan bush pilots. They fly year round supporting people and are like arteries to the body, carrying the needed supplies to Alaska's southwest. Among these past fearless fliers were the well-known, such as John Bishops and Ted Maroney. Courageous as they were, they continually flew to the mountains and coastal villages, carrying passengers and supplies. They were experienced old-time fliers, professionals who landed small Super Cubs with skis on mountain glaciers and switched to huge tires to land on sandy beaches of the ocean coast.

Both men are now a part of that natural beauty, paving the way for others: a new breed of bush pilots who continue to fly above the migrating herds of caribou and increasing human population. Some of the new pilots still have daily routines that take them to the glaciers and beaches, supplying equipment and food to climbers or naturalists. Many fly to the rough strips made of dirt and gravel. The job is still very risky. Most of the natives greet the pilots with friendly smiles, a shake of the hand, and a cup of coffee. One never knows when a turn may come for a life-saving medevac, the only hope for a critically injured patient.

To Wayne Carpenter, one of these Alaskan pilots, flying was a passion and a way of life. No matter where there was a need, Wayne and his airplane would take on the wrath of Mother Nature regardless of the lurking fury of the unfriendly skies above. Noted for his kind and quick-witted humor, along with his calm, patient demeanor, and his professional attitude set him apart from the others as the top pilot in the area. As an experienced U.S. Air Force combat pilot, the root of his attitude and flying mannerisms, he had been nicknamed "Hammer" for his aggressive behavior. In time, that aggressive attitude, once used in the war zones of Vietnam, changed. The result was a more mature and sophisticated aviator. Combining the product of battle experience, plus a respect for Mother Nature, Hammer's formula for success was created. He had another side, different from the "all-work tough guy" façade, his usual guise. During occasional rough or difficult flights, Hammer would be reminded of the past; revealing displaced emotions once thought to be forgotten. His experience, flying in a hostile environment, was triggered revealing actions learned in war; Hammer possessed the desire to help the unfortunate or forgotten. These feelings of fair play were obvious to others and inspired and created admiration to follow his lead, helping the less fortunate and his fellow veterans who had been neglected or overlooked seemed his hidden agenda.

Carpenter's territory was focused between Anchorage and Dutch Harbor, providing air transportation for people and cargo. Although a slow transformation has been taking place, replacing many of the gravel strips with hard surfaces, concrete, or asphalt, smaller planes are still required for access to the many smaller villages. His small fleet of Cessna 336s was known throughout the region and so was his reliability. Some flew with him just to say, "I flew with a true hero and a legend in the aviation field." Others just needed the reliable service that Hammer offered. His company was based in the small town of Dillingham, Alaska, overlooking Bristol Bay where he once lived with his family.

The story you are about to embark upon is one that takes Hammer's already adventurous lifestyle of flying to an intriguing chase, both mentally and physically taxing. Forced to take action against a diabolical enemy, his thoughts were only of his family, his best friend, and his country; little did he know of the lurking dangers from an unknown terrorist threat. Hammer was infuriated by the violence toward his best friend, and his family was threatened. They would always be in danger if he did nothing. They would be targets for those brutal, lawless terrorists who had no regard for human life or law in this country. Hammer used his experience and knowledge to find and fight an unknown enemy, one exceeding even his wildest imagination. There was no room for carelessness; the result would be death.

The thought of his best friend, Bill, being in danger festered in his mind and his reaction to the situation, not knowing the enemy, left him few options. He would use his training and experience, plus his gut instinct, to prepare for retaliation. What would be the repercussions from his actions? Hammer had no alternative but to organize a team of experts who knew the most modern ways of tactical warfare, using technology and intelligence gathering far above his ability. For this mission, one of skirting the outer boundaries of the law, this type of team was needed.

This story is familiar to me because I was part of the information-gathering process. I also took part in the apprehension of the cell, witnessing Hammer's fierce and tenacious ability to take action against the unknown and deal with the threats to his loved ones. It was a task that most people would never knowingly take on. With the borders of the United States free and entry into the country a simple task, there will always be the possibility of threats from those who want to disrupt or destroy the ideals for which this free country stands. Hammer had already fought years to protect many of these ideals.

The events in these files reveal the heroism of a few that saved many. It is composed from interviews and documentation compiled during and after forming "the team." It was my privilege to have worked with and known both Hammer and Bill.

Dennis A. Maxwell

D/D CIA Langley

PROLOGUE

Mark felt that he was being excessively punished, as if he was a child being sent to his room. He was, as he walked the terminal at the international. Occasionally he snuck a glimpse through the windows, showing his frustration with chills, the shrug of shoulders, and a sigh. Mother Nature was not helping. Her presence in Anchorage was demonstrated by an ability to form a low overcast that shielded the sun, releasing a flurry of half rain, half snow. The ground remained covered with a white half-frozen sloppy slush with a four- to six-foot barrier of ice having been piled in the middle of the roadways. A state more than half surrounded by water and known for its rugged mountains and crappy weather, Alaska had a population of more bear, caribou, moose and deer than human beings. At least Mark was thankful with just having to deal with the smaller human population.

With fewer people in the city, one would have thought there would be an absence of sounds or snarled traffic, but this was not the case. Anchorage is not a small city. The frenzy of cluttered sidewalks and streets may not be to the extent of a New York, San Francisco or even Seattle, but the population that does exist is constantly on the move.

To Mark and his begrudging and pity-filled way of thinking, this strange, undesirable city had not been in his foreseeable future. More of an unreal fantasy, he had a hard time conjuring up the fact that he was actually here! Was this a bad dream? His recently acquired frustrated tone was from having to leave the Midwest, and not by choice. He would much rather be in sunny, warm Los Angeles, some two thousand miles to the south, or even back in St. Louis. The rain and wind presented a hard start to a difficult job; his attitude stunk.

The morning of his demise was still clear in his mind, being summoned to the chief's office on that ominously cloudy and threatening day, rain being an obvious precursor to an unwanted but somewhat expected assignment or even termination. He settled his nerves by thinking about the upcoming afternoon of warmth on the tennis courts at the local university, impressing the young eligible ladies with his forehand.

Setting his USC mug on his desk, half-filled with the tepid remains of a vanilla mocha that had lost most of its froth and was covered with a layer of slimy whipped cream, he wondered what lay ahead after last week's debacle. Mark sauntered to the chief's back office, a wood and glass structure. The secluded office was located under a back stairwell, the stairs leading to the more important offices in the FBI, one story above. He had only been up there once before, and at the rate things were happening he would never be a permanent resident.

He knocked and entered to the appearance of his chief's snarly tempestuous, but smoothly shaven face. The face belonged to the bureaus first in command of the Midwest region department who specialized in terrorism. The chief raised his head slightly as Mark entered and shut the door. "Ah! Glenrose! I have a special assignment just up your alley, a chance to impress the deputy director and get back in good graces with the department."

Crap! Deep down, Mark knew that fortunately there were no field offices in the mountains of the Himalayas or on the beaches of Wake Island. If there were, he would surely be packing in the assumption of heading there. With the chief's tone, he wondered what could be the worst assignment ever. In essence, his previous thoughts wouldn't be too far off.

His boss continued in a steady machine-like, unemotional manner. "The unit supervisor in Anchorage has requested assistance with a special team working some shipping problems in that area. There were rumors and scuttlebutt from various ship captains and trucking operators of arms and equipment apparently being transported through Alaska to various ports in the lower forty-eight. A new team of agents has been assembled and are investigating without any success. With your experience, the team would benefit. This was about as clear as Anchorage made it. I told them I would send an experienced agent and that's where you come in. Good luck."

The boss finished by handing him a folder with his contact information and at the same time moved his hand toward the door. He never did show any acknowledgement to Glenrose and said nothing else. He was finished as he refocused back down on the papers on his desk. Mark realized he was finished too!

Mark quietly and dejectedly replied to unhearing ears, "I'll get my things together," knowing there was no good reason for objecting to the inevitable. There was still no sound or movement from the boss, who now seemed like a statue behind a desk. He turned and silently walked out of the office with most of the confidence missing from his once cocky step. This unit wanted him out, and Anchorage was his punishment for a job poorly done. What he didn't see was his boss shaking his head as the door shut behind him. That was not a good sign.

Brainwashed to take the brunt of the blame, Mark was embarrassed by the department, threatened with lawsuits and by the families of a few foreign nationals who all wanted his hide. It was perfectly clear that the situation was made to be purely *his* fault. By the demeaning treatment he suffered daily and being continually chastised by his coworkers, he knew he was lucky to avert this failure without losing his job.

His demise was the result of being the head of an STU, a Specialized Terrorist Unit in St. Louis. The unit had uncovered names, facts, leaders and actually the complete cell, an operation taking many man hours at an enormous expense. But after planning and perfectly executing the operation, the unit failed to indict anyone. The buildings had been empty and any trace of a terrorist cell seemed to vanish. They had always been one step ahead of his every move. The al-Qaeda cell had moved and relocated to some unknown area just before the unit raided the businesses. One of a few suspected family stores that had been under surveillance as a front turned out to be just that: a family-operated "ma and pa" grocery mart.

The warrants were not hard to secure, even with trivial and pitiful evidence. Personal injuries and damages from the searches of suspected persons, property, and buildings were significant. What's worse was the fact that no evidence of explosives or weaponry had been found. The entire unit's efforts, as it was, without an ounce of ammunition, grenades, machineguns, explosives, or shipping manifests to show, was a bust; a waste of time, money and manpower. Most of all, the incursion could not be scored in the win or success column credited to the FBI.

The snickers from Homeland Security could be heard from the east coast to the west. The cost of the effort, the ensuing court battles, and the all important embarrassment to the department was Mark's undoing. Even more so, he was charged with careless execution and timing of each individual aspect of the operation. There was never a reprieve. The whole department suffered the wrath of lawyers, public scrutiny, and competing agencies.

Mark was also the cause of "the phone call," that one historic call to his department and his supervisor from the director himself. The things that were said; "I expected more than a loose ship", "you are the responsible one" and finally, "the time might have come for replacements", turned the chief red and sweat covered, lips scalloped and ears pulled back. His supervisor was a raging moose when he appeared from his office. Mark figured he had about two days left with the bureau.

This was his tenth day since the chief had given him his ticket to cross the River Styx, the fourteenth from "the phone call," as he opened a taxi door and hopped in to get dry and head for downtown Anchorage. He expected to see Charon, in his hooded cape full of bones, driving the cab. Once in Anchorage, things should have been looking up. At least he wasn't fired, but Anchorage? The only thing he saw and felt when he looked up was rain blowing sideways. Maybe he should quit!

Mark met with the Anchorage bureau chief and they sparred with eyes at first, followed with the typical jabs and innuendos. He didn't mind that the conversation started out with introductions and then the statement, "Who did you piss off?" They both chuckled and he explained how he got there. His new chief warmed to Mark, realizing Mark wasn't there after his job, and informed him that he was not the only other agent to come up to Alaska not of his own free will. In fact, another of Mark's team members from St. Louis was also being sent up and would be joining him, helping "find and capture the elusive gunrunners," as the chief put it. Mark noticed the tone of sarcasm but, decided to ignore it. He had other things on his mind and didn't know just exactly the amount of doo-doo he was in.

For Mark, his petty little dislikes for his situation were just that, minor, compared to what he would soon have to endure. Mark would eventually find out just how vast the state of Alaska was and the difficulty he would have finding that proverbial "needle in the haystack" when it didn't want to be found.

Mark was given an office and an assistant and was formally introduced to his new unit, a young group of agents just out of the academy, eager to get their hands dirty and solve cases. Thinking to himself, these newbie's were here "Either to solve cases or prove themselves for a better position in the lower forty-eight". Muttering to himself had been a new practice in the past few weeks.

Later in the day, with the help of his assistant, he found a perfect little apartment on the east side of Lake Hood with a westerly view overlooking the lake. He could make out the international airport through the deciduous trees to the south. Being a private pilot and still having that eagerness of wanting to watch every plane that went by, he would have the opportunity to observe the big, tubby Japanese 747 airliners landing. They appeared slow on approach with everything sticking out: slats, flaps, spoilers, speed brakes, doors, clam shells, gear, and whatever else they could shove out to slow them down. He could also watch the smaller planes, more his speed, flying over head to or from Lake Hood or other facilities in the area.

Reporting the next day to the three-story dirty gray building in downtown Anchorage, Mark was basically on his own. He knew he had to start this assignment in a better frame of mind than his present attitude dictated. He gave way to the fact that Anchorage would be his residence for the next umpteen months and knew that the more successful he became, the less time he would have to wait for a transfer.

He readied himself for the day with coffee, a banana, and a granola bar—light, perfect nourishment for the task of getting to know the members of his unit. At first he would spoon-feed methods and analyze and oversee all of the information the team members had accumulated so far. His one advantage in Anchorage was bringing a fresh view of FBI protocol. What to look for and how to organize the facts was his forte. Most of all, his experience was what might save him from "this place!" The teams were anxious and willing to learn from an experienced agent who knew terrorism. Now, if he could only get used to the damp, cold weather, his attitude might improve.

Even though he had been in the building for an hour, Mark was still cold and feeling soaked when he walked into the board room and his new unit. His first statement set the mood and indicated his displeasure with the entire situation. "Does the wind and rain ever stop up here?"

His low, raspy voice questioned the onlookers in their rain-soaked clothes and windblown hair. Subtle, courteous laughter followed from the agents, who knew the feeling and wanted to stay in good graces with their new boss. At least he still had some humor. His subconscious thoughts were displacing any necessary business at hand, replacing them with images of the sunny beaches of LA and the tennis courts of St. Louis he loved. His rebellious thoughts, loving nothing here, would have to be cast aside for his survival. It was time for him to start filling in the hole that he had dug for himself in the bureau if he ever wanted to get out of this predicament.

PART 1

CAT AND MOUSE

The Demise of the Infidels

Chapter 1

The day was windy, the usual ten to fifteen knots with gusts up to twenty-five, and choppy due to currents of air bouncing off hills and land structures that were being fed from high-velocity ocean air. The shape of the panhandle and the peninsula that form the Gulf of Alaska helps generate, capture, and guide numerous highs and lows into a natural catch basin, one providing an environment for the ultimate flying challenge. Wind was never unusual for southwest Alaska. The sky was mostly cloud-filled and with a 3,000-foot ceiling rapidly moving northeasterly, all was gray and white with an occasional patch of blue. The puffy white vapor characterized unstable low-pressure clouds, with winds moving in a counterclockwise direction from the center of the system located a hundred miles out in the gulf. The low created an onshore flow across the narrow width of the peninsula and up the Cook Inlet.

To Hammer, comfort was just being in a plane. Wind was wind and he was under control, with his muscles powered by a bit of adrenaline and that last cup of coffee. Conditions of heavy winds, known as "common" to this part of the world, were his forte. He embraced the airplane, caressing the yoke and peddles in synchronization, guiding the machine to an exact location. Once in a while his head would impact the interior of the plane from an unexpected bump of excessive turbulence. There was no thought of panic or fear, just a gentle tightening of the belts. His touch was from years of experience gained from time spent "in country," the old military phrase, depicting the time spent in an environment mostly hostile. The term "hostile" also suited Alaska perfectly.

Flying and landing the Cessna Skymaster was hardly ever a problem for him. The airplane would fly in just about any weather but ice. Landings, however, were tricky. There was a suggested sixteen-knot maximum crosswind component assigned to the smaller twin engine Cessna airplane, which occasionally was exceeded. Besides the wind, sharp fist-sized gravel and chuck holes the size of bathtubs covered the runway, which an occasional caribou scampered across; it was a wonder that he did not spend more time straightening landing gear.

At first, when he had just started flying out of Dillingham and the area was all new to him, the adrenaline high would not necessarily be overbearing, but noticeable from the sweat running down his face. This happened to everyone in the first few weeks of flying this area. Stress and fatigue from having filled the day with too many hours of flying caused Hammer's experiences in Vietnam to occasionally reappear. Justifying any thoughts of insanity, he rationalized that most of the time he considered himself quite stable, but as with any veteran who had flown in combat conditions the mind sometimes played games with mental visions when triggered.

On occasion, images of 'nam would flash in his mind, reminding him of the damage to his airplane from low-level passes, a product of bullets and tree limbs. Over there, nasty rain squalls would continually create zero visibility, keeping him guessing to the whereabouts of any landing strips. In that time of aviation history, there was no GPS. The bulldozed patches of reddish dirt, covered sporadically with metal matting and showing no threshold marks for a beginning or end, was the place he used for a temporary nest for his bird. With the difficult flying conditions in 'nam and the usual damage to the aircraft, trying to not be a statistic and falling short or landing long of the runway, made touchdown challenging. The jungle always had things flying out and the sloppy, reddish mud runways, splashing and spraying thick goo that covered the airplane, made the whole experience demanding every single flight, every single day.

Thirty years after 'nam, thoughts and images of battle were few and the passing of time and each new flight out of Dillingham refreshing. One thing he looked forward to was the absence of bullet holes on his post flight checks; in 'nam, he was continually covering them but here, not having to perform the ritual of patching, made for a much more satisfying flight. There were always other things out to get him. Daydreaming or lackadaisical feelings were two silent enemies of fliers; overconfidence and complacency were two more. A few deep breaths from the overhead air vent and a glance out of the fuselage to diagnose the direction and conditions of the wind put Hammer in the ready mode for any situation. Landings were anything but normal and depended on the circumstances, such as crosswinds, rain, and unannounced traffic. There was a list fifty deep. The pilot had to be ahead of the airplane, knowing what was going to happen before it happened, and had to know the airport. Hammer had that all important 100 percent concentration on what he was required to do.

Most of the damage to the airplanes in the bush was not only from rough runways, but from nasty gusts of wind at touchdown causing a side load on the gear. This is why he preferred the straight-leg 336 rather than the 337, a retract; the hydraulic system for the retractable landing gear was more delicate on the 337, and it would only take that one time to not have the gear extend to ruin his whole day.

In the wet season, the runways were not oozing sloppy mud, but mostly gravel that drained well. The gravel could be groomed to eliminate the large chuck holes. The danger of the gravel was during the thaw, when it deep freezes in the winter, sometimes as much as a foot and a half deep, and then thawed in the spring. The result was a process of a solid changing to a liquid. As the ground and gravel thawed, it was like chocolate pudding a foot thick. The slop might last just a few weeks or a month and a half, depending on the temperature and rain. Hammer convinced the townspeople with runways to keep their vehicles off the surface during that time. This was to keep from getting ten- to twelve-inch deep ruts.

He did not want to be like the Air Force crews that spent hours cleaning mud from landing gear and engines every day. A ding in a prop from a rock was costly. Unlike military aircraft, any damage came out of profits and surely was not paid for by Uncle Sam. Without a good operating machine, heaven forbid the failure of any mechanical part in flight. The journey for survival in the case of ditching would lead most assuredly to death.

With only two of the 336 Cessna's working in his company fleet, repair was still a daily chore. He had been so busy, time for repair of the third plane, lying in a heap of unrecognizable parts and covered by canvas at the side of the hangar in Anchorage, had been limited. That was a reminder for him not to hire unproven pilots. The constant abuse, the normal wear and tear on tires from gravel strips and the usual aircraft inspections made maintenance a large part of the day. If the aircraft needed fixing it was attended to and, along with the required fifty-hour progressive maintenance checks, Hammer's evening entertainment was set.

Hammer was a fanatic about maintenance. One of his philosophies was to make "a good and thorough walk around before flight." If one was to ignore or miss a part of that all-important preflight ritual, one was apt to be a statistic and it was easy for the Alaskan bush country to consume any airplane. After all, if the fan stopped, it stopped and the reason didn't matter. You were still going down. That was why two engines were best. No one else was going to check the plane out and he was not in the military any longer with eyes of others and all the work done for him.

Hammer became a master at reading Mother Nature's weather signs. He watched for any wind speed or directional changes using water or "people" signs like smoke or flags. Low clouds and precipitation were always hiding hills and cliffs. In the vicinity of some small villages, restricted visibility prevented animals or people from vacating the short rough runways in a timely manner. They could hear, but not see and that could cause a go-around, a maneuver that cost fuel and time. To help make normal landings, a landing so that the airplane could be used again for flight, an additional item was placed on his Gas, Undercarriage (landing gear), Manifold pressure and Prop check (an abbreviated landing checklist). That item was an extra O meaning "On your toes, Bucko!" Landing was not a place to be half asleep.

Ice in the air was a big factor. Freezing temperatures occurred from the ground up in early fall to late spring and with the surrounding nearby water adding to the mix, *voila!* Ice. This was why Alaska was known as one of the most challenging places to fly.

Lake Iliamna was near hills and some smaller mountains that produced unusual weather, causing the winds to funnel through the valleys and to be orographically lifted, forming more clouds and precipitation. This is much like the way it is all over southwest Alaska. At the mouth of Kamishak Bay, just south of Iliamna, the large mass of water supported a reputation of high, unstable winds and turbulent conditions.

The wind was near twenty-two knots when the day's flight started early in the morning. For Hammer, as he departed from Dillingham carrying a few passengers to Anchorage, the trip was routine. On the turn around, a plane load of boat parts was needed for the fishing fleet at Port Heiden along with several government packages for the FAA. Port Heiden was a small community between King Salmon and Cold Bay on the northern side of the peninsula.

The last leg of the trip was a load of ice, fresh fruit, bakery goods, and spirits for the lodge, the Iliamna Fishing Guide Service, on the southwest end of Lake Iliamna. Bill Rankowski, the owner and Hammer's best friend, had some special customers in for a couple of weeks and needed extra supplies. The King Salmon Commercial Company, just across from the airport at King Salmon, would have the supplies ready for pick-up when he landed. Hammer had informed Bill, "No problem, I got you covered." Once said by Hammer, Bill, or any other customer, for that matter, could feel assured that the cargo would be there on time! The flow of the trip, not having to back track, would not cause much extra air time and minimal money for extra fuel. Hammer thought nothing of helping his friend and had agreed to finish his flight for the day with the delivery, followed by the short trip home.

In the past, Bill had helped Hammer when his friends had come up from the lower forty-eight for some fishing and relaxing. There was no one better than Bill to guide them to the large fish. The reputation of the lodge for fishing and the native cuisine brought dinning enthusiasts in from all over the state, mostly from the nearby communities. Some came from as far away as Anchorage when openings were available.

"I have a limited amount of time with my schedule. I can't hang around," Hammer had told Bill over a week ago when arrangements had been made. He hoped Bill would understand. There was an important engagement this evening that he had to attend. Amanda, Hammer's number two daughter, would be extremely upset if her one and only parent were to miss another of her performances. An hour or so flight would not make much of a difference in time; it was just the idle chit-chat at the lake that usually caused the tardiness.

For Hammer and his active lifestyle, always on the go, his compulsory tasks were seldom different. There was always the maintenance, being ready for business, sustaining a reputation so people would have faith in his service, and the family. The family activities were not second by any means, but his daughters had to understand he was the owner of an important, and in some instances a life-sustaining, business.

To his daughters, their activities were far more important than the smelly old hangar or the funny looking airplanes. During a past weekend, Hammer had spent long, hard hours turning wrenches, completing the fifty-hour inspections on the planes, replacing a few worn-out parts and a front engine right-side magneto. It took longer than he had expected and he lost track of time, affecting other plans he had made. He noticed that both engines on his most used plane were getting long on time and would soon have to be replaced. All of the maintenance had to be done on the second plane before he flew it to British Columbia for a much needed new paint job.

Maintenance was the only way to keep an engine running and get as much time out of them as possible. Hammer had tried to explain the situation, as he had many times before, but to his daughter, the engine work was unimportant. His number one daughter had a late afternoon volleyball game that he had missed and she would not forgive his absence for any reason. Hammer kept explaining that the planes had to be reliable and ready to fly. They were the source for food on the table. There could be no shortcuts for maintenance. She knew this, but the tears said it all.

Company policy was that their flights would operate at any time and about any place on the peninsula. The planes would fly to most of the populated areas of the state, anywhere they could land, that is, except on the beaches, especially the saltwater. The surface of the beach was often soft and eventually the saltwater caused destructive corrosion. There were larger scheduled companies that generally flew to the farther destinations at a lesser price. Carpenter Air would not compete with them. His competition was with the smaller aircraft. The advantage of Hammer's service was having few competitors with the size of aircraft he used. His aircraft had two engines for safety, which many passengers appreciated.

Hammer had his own rules to follow and wanted to offer his clients a company that promoted customer needs as well as safety. That also included the fact that he wasn't afraid to sit out a nasty front of turbulent air and rain squalls, opting for a more comfortable flight. It made for a good opportunity to be on the ground with a cup of coffee, reading about what was happening in the world instead off bouncing around the inside of the plane like a ping-pong ball pinging off the walls of a clothes dryer. For some flights, being on the ground rather than flying in the rough stuff, waiting for the weather to pass, it would actually save maintenance time. He would have to add the cost of cleaning the puke from an airsick passenger or passengers to the other items on the "to do" list. He was noted for being a compassionate pilot and one to have concern for his passengers. Flying was very competitive and an excellent reputation was required. In his area of operation, he had accomplished just that.

Other pilots that worked in the same general location spoke highly of his company. He was proud of this fact and wanted to maintain a respected reputation, one already known throughout Alaska and as far south as Seattle and Denver.

The airplane he flew, 78 Bravo, was showing signs of engine problems. There had been nothing definitive to worry about until the trip from Port Heiden to King Salmon. Hammer noticed a definite drop in RPMs and a loss of power from a rough-running magneto on the rear engine. If there had been any possibility of risk to passengers, Hammer would not have made the trip. However, he could easily make it to Dillingham by himself. If it weren't for the fact that the second plane was now on its way to British Columbia for a new paint job, he would have switched.

On this last leg of the trip, Hammer kept alert for the short private strip near the lodge, just up the bank above Lake Iliamna. He would probably see smoke from the lodge before the strip. Bill had purchased an old grader, left at one of the older strips nearby that was salvageable. He hired a Sikorsky Sky Crane to lift and move it to his strip. Bill took pleasure mounting the contraption with the large blade and smoothing the pot holes. He mostly graded the short strip for the customers' convenience, not the pilot's, providing a better pad for soft landings.

As Hammer grew closer to the lake, his final drop-off for the day, he made a call to the lodge about fifteen miles out. It produced nothing but silence. "That wasn't typical of Bill. Was the old guy sleeping?" Hammer thought whimsically, knowing that Bill was only a few months older than him. Hammer kidded Bill as being much older and wiser, but had nothing but respect for him. They often talked about the old times in 'nam and the secretive special ops Bill had been assigned to. The two were like brothers. He tried again, "Iliamna lodge, this is 78 Bravo." There was still no answer.

Since Bill didn't answer the radio, Hammer figured the next best thing would be a buzz job and that's exactly what he did. When Hammer wanted someone's attention, he was really good at the task. He wouldn't fly close enough to knock on the door, but he was able to count the roofing nails on the metal roof. At seventy-five feet over the top of the lodge and at 150 knots, the effect inside was thunderous.

"That's what Bill gets for not answering back", he thought. Bill must have been out fishing with clients. Hammer turned 78 Bravo toward the "final," using a bush traffic pattern, and lined up the airplane about the center of the runway. He applied a bit of left aileron into the wind and left rudder for a forward slip to maintain position to the runway. A last glance, he judged the white caps and water spray for wind direction and velocity. "Must be a little over twenty knots and off the nose to the left" was his best guess. The air was a little choppy. Reducing power and adding flaps, he slowed the plane down for a nice soft touchdown on the left wheel first, and then the right. The landing was perfect and Hammer back-taxied 78B to the turn-around on the northeast side of the runway and shut down the engines.

Quickly releasing his shoulder harness and belt, he flipped the master and ignition switch to off. He was halfway out the door by the time the props stopped turning, expecting Bill to be waiting for him. He was always there, but for some reason he wasn't today.

Unloading the items and wrapping them in pieces of canvas, Hammer placed the bundles in an old wooden ice box near the supply shed right next to where he had taxied. He hustled back to the plane and started her up. There was still no sign of Bill. He hoped everything was okay.

Hammer didn't seem to notice the vehicle behind a small airport building a hundred yards away, with two men watching every move. At least he didn't react to seeing them. It was not until taking off and a turn back over the runway for another fly over that Hammer saw the two men who were now loading the vehicle with the supplies he had left. Something was not right and he reacted by critical observation and acting natural, perhaps a habit of combat. He used a rapid eye scan to observe every detail of the lodge, trying to memorize every inch of what was happening. So far Bill wasn't working the radio on the way out either.

Another good buzz was in order to let them know at the lodge to pick up their supplies. In the short time it took to turn about, the men in the vehicle had finished loading and were under way to the lodge. Hammer needed a better look. No need to break the routine either. He was sure that Bill could not have missed the first fly-by, but maybe a new rule for a second had to be established. Hammer chuckled at the idea. This pass was strictly to see if Bill might be in trouble. As the twin boom, high-wing aircraft with two high revved engines passed over the lodge, Hammer noticed a number of people stationed around the building. It looked like a tightly guarded compound near Saigon. "What's all of this about?" Hammer said to himself. He tried the radio once more. "Iliamna Fish and Guide, this is 78 Bravo."

At the click of the mike, Bill answered, "Thanks for the drop. Out."

The program was probably going to be "Swan Lake" or "Cinderella," something musical to keep third, fourth and fifth graders prancing and dancing and the parents googly, teary-eyed, in an "ah" cuteness. Once was enough for him to endure. That once was with Jackie, the oldest at just fifteen. There should be some kind of law that a parent only had to watch these activities once. In Hammer's mind, real entertainment was watching professional linebackers go about their business rather than musicals and dancing. Looking your opponent in the eye and getting ready to smack him in the kisser with as much force as one could muster was much more to his pleasure than cutesy little dances. Fifth graders were tolerable, but going through the process of finding a seat, being next to the rest of the parents and having to be pleasant, looking sincere and "ooing and ahhing" as the program continued was too much! A good soccer match or a basketball game from the older girls was at least stimulating enough to stay awake. Supporting the girls was a parent's requirement, but that didn't help his feeling of being doomed for the evening. At least one of the two girls was dad's little girl and liked the airplanes. Jackie also liked to kick the daylights out of the soccer ball.

Hammer had a lot on his mind with his girls, the planes, the business and now the lodge situation. He thought, "Why was the lodge guarded?" His thoughts swirled around his head. Bill always wanted to talk. Hammer couldn't think of any reason for that many guards. With so many people around, there was no need to worry about bears. Black bears would certainly stay away from as many people as were standing outside of the lodge. How come Bill didn't call on the radio after the first low-level buzz? The two of them had been earning a living in this area for years and Bill always wanted to talk. Hammer rationalized by thinking that Bill had probably been busy and trusted that the supplies would be delivered. What about those two in the car?

A mix of impulses and synapses firing created thoughts that were too much in his state of tiredness. He was perplexed about a decision to honor his commitment to his daughter or find out what was going on at the lodge. A simple phone call couldn't just alert a policeman to drive by and look in on what was probably nothing. The lodge was in the boonies, out in "no man's land." He was feeling punchy, frustrated and helpless. Hammer wasn't a young man anymore, but refused to slow down and not think through every little detail that was firing in his brain. Most importantly, was his friend in trouble?

Leaning 78 Bravo out at 4,500 feet and heading for Dillingham, it was a good time to fly. The winds were settling and the daylight was starting to fade. Once back at the hangar there would be plenty of time to change that persistent rough-running magneto that had plagued the trip since before King Salmon. Hopefully there would be parts on the shelf in the hangar that might work. If not, he would have to call in an order and get a part on a plane for tomorrow's flight from Anchorage. He hated the thought of having his plane grounded if there was no magneto or parts for a rebuild.

Why do parents think that involving kids in ballet, or any other activity, for that matter, is something the kids liked? Half the time they were made fools of and, if older, resented the fact that they were even involved. Hammer didn't really hate going to these shows, he only went because his wife would have wanted him to. Subconsciously, he didn't want the image of being a "tough guy" in doubt. When the oldest daughter was going through the same age, it was fun and entertaining, but now it was a chore and reminded him of the good times with his wife, Suzanne. The stress and nervousness was evident to both the performers and the parents, hoping for the best for their children and for a performance with no mistakes. However, there were always mistakes and sometimes tears. There had to be a way to miss the performance. Hammer's mind was once again bouncing back and forth from ballet to Bill to airplane parts. The least of his thoughts were concentrating on flying.

Nearing the end of the trip, the outline of Dillingham was becoming visible, the magneto had been getting rougher and Hammer had shut it down; better off than on. Only ten minutes out and with power less than normal, flying was still a breeze compared to that time near Kontum in "nam, with the rear engine shot out and a rough-running forward engine. Hammer smiled and thought, "Thank goodness for altitude." He cheated Murphy that day.

Cinderella might be okay, but not another Swan Lake. Hammer winced at the thought of the spinning and high-kicking fifth graders. The full outline of buildings surrounding Dillingham was just starting to appear and he made a second radio call to airport advisory to let other pilots know where he was. The landing was made and 78 Bravo taxied to the hangar. The only worries Hammer thought of now would be staying awake to the sounds of a piano and high–pitched, out-of-tune voices.

A quick check for a spare magneto found that there were no parts on his stock shelf to replace the bad one, so Hammer dialed the phone number of Mid Alaskan Aviation and placed an order for a next-day delivery. The airplane had to be working as soon as possible. There might be enough parts for a rebuild on the shelf, but after another quick scan, not even a rebuild was likely. He had no idea what the problem was and would have to take the mag apart for diagnosis. Hammer remembered he had used the spares the previous weekend. All of his rummaging around and preparation, trying to keep his planes able and airworthy, having the necessary parts available, finally came to a halt and he realized for the first time that he would be without a usable airplane until the new part arrived. This is why he had two. Three would have been nice, but it was just the circumstance.

With no plane and a tired and defeated attitude, Hammer called his friend, dialing the number of the lodge at Iliamna on his sat phone. On the third ring Bill answered. At least it sounded like Bill. Hammer asked if he received the supplies and if everything was all right. Bill replied, "Everything's fine." Hammer then asked him about the men around the lodge. The reply was a click and then silence. "We must have been cut off," Hammer muttered. "Oh well, at least Bill was there."

The dancing wasn't too bad and the girls knew the reward would be ice cream, a big hit with both of them. The two were happy it was the weekend and after the program and a quick family discussion, they decided to go out for a movie and some pizza. But then Hammer had a better idea and made the offer: the satellite dish, some home-baked pizza and followed by some good old fashion "Neapolitan ice cream bars. Sandy, Hammer's sister, had a date so it would just be he and the girls. Hammer thought that with his luck, the movie they chose would probably be *Cinderella*. Maybe he could justify some repairs in the hangar after all.

The next morning Hammer wasn't awakened by dreams of tutus, but by a call from Jim Gibson of Mid Alaskan Aviation, the aircraft parts supplier he used. It was 8:00 A.M. and Gibson was gathering parts to be shipped out. The clerk had scribbled a number he couldn't read so he wanted to confirm the correct part numbers. He also wanted to know if Hammer wanted a Slick or Bendix magnito. He would have to cross-reference the Slick. MAA was a conscientious company and would rather not send the wrong parts out. One of the larger scheduled carriers had a plane due in to Dillingham at 11:30 A.M. with the part promised to be aboard. This was the way an aircraft was kept flyable in the bush. Sometimes larger companies helped the smaller, a more or less symbiotic relationship.

Chapter 2

Seated around a rectangular table, the members of Mark's unit were listening to their specific assignments as they were broken into teams of two and given areas to investigate. With disappointment in his tone, feeling the displeasure of reviewing what little progress and fact finding his unit had made so far, Mark started rattling off "the way he wanted the information gathered" as he wrote the words on his white board. Rooting out and finding any significant movement of arms and names of people or companies, including just plain scuttlebutt, were the bare minimum expectations for his agents. He displayed an outline, his method of a typical board of sequence and a means of informing the other teams, displaying factual significant material useful to all. He also used a large monitor with a PowerPoint presentation he had created to show a step-by-step procedure for this system. If nothing else, Mark was organized.

Mark, at first, was amazed with the amount of information that had been collected. There was no organization, no particular strategy for investigation, and all was arranged in piles of folders in cardboard boxes. He felt like each and every agent was on his own, circling around the pool of the Alaskan population like a school of fish in a pond, waiting for the rains to come and the worms to follow. Organization and computer technology were his strengths. He also knew that the bureau had spent a lot of money training the agents to do better work than he had seen so far. If they wanted to find the proverbial "pot of gold," then they had better look in other places than under a rainbow. The unit's time had been mostly a total waste and without direction. He would certainly cure this problem.

An amazing fact to Mark was the amount of area the agents would have to cover. A large wall map, labeled with pins that signified where he would send the different teams or where they had already been, hung just to the left of his desk. The area from Fairbanks west-southwest to Dutch Harbor and farther was a distance of a thousand miles or more. Many more pinholes would be needed before he would be satisfied. He wanted what he could not have. There was no significant road structure like in St. Louis. Except for locally, from Fairbanks west to Anchorage and Kenai to Homer, driving was impossible. The journey to Kodiak, all the way to Dutch, could be made by boat, but the unit had no time for even a one-way trip. The bureau did not have its own plane. All of the teams, except the local ones, would have to use commercial air travel. This created a problem of concealment. The ability of the teams to remain anonymous in the small communities was in doubt. It would be like holding a sign up on Main Street saying, "The FBI is in town." Small villages and towns, some with fewer than a hundred people, would all know if strangers were in their communities and automatically send the red flag of suspicion flying, even if they did not intend to do so.

Mark had high hopes for his unit now that he was under control, and he knew their failure was also his. After all, he was a veteran of many years and new the ways of the al-Qaeda from his stint in St. Louis. He would have liked to have had "success" in St. Louis but knew better than to bring up that subject. There was no fooling him; this assignment was billed to be a slough-off, when actually the amount of work to be done was enormous. He also assumed that those still interested in his failure were keeping an eye out for any of his unit's shortcomings. Perhaps this would be his undoing. Perhaps Anchorage would be his last assignment.

In pairs, Mark's agents were released, each to a specific location to investigate certain people and businesses that fit profiles and reasonable means of transportation that could be used for smuggling. Mark had relayed his concerns, hoping a solid understanding of the tasks each team faced became critical in their thinking; by the time everyone had left, he felt in firm control. His starting point for success had been established and he was confident that the success of his unit would prevail, finding, if any, all possible terrorist activities. His mood was changing and a twinge of thought, a slightly hazy image of sun and tennis courts, began to appear. Shaking his head to the present, he caught himself before the daydream took over and he became all business again.

Alone and thinking of what he would do if he was to transport arms and explosives, Mark decided to spend time mapping and laying out known transport companies on his office wall, separating the existing files of material in an orderly and easily usable manor to indicate possible suspects. He would certainly give himself a few days to interpret the material and associate it to known companies on the "watch list." If, indeed, there was a movement of weapons taking place, he, if anybody, would find where the arms were coming from or being shipped to. He hadn't understood the chief's cynical attitude when he had first arrived, but now he understood the skepticism and how it related to his task. So far, the poor organization and fact finding attempts, lack of funds and inexperienced attitudes all contributed to a stacked deck and he knew it. He also knew he was no novice investigator and would show these backwoods hicks the way the big boys played. Mark's confidence was growing again. He knew his capabilities and was anything but a rookie. His "watch list" would grow and his teams would succeed.

Wayne Carpenter, known by friends and family as "Hammer" for continually tackling and pounding everyone and anything with his head at age two, was born and raised in Colorado Springs, Colorado. His father was an ordinary man who worked as a civilian mechanic on the army base at Fort Carson. He worked long, hard hours repairing heavy machinery. He spent his off time with his family and his true love, football, most notably watching Ray Nitschke and Dick Butkus. He also loved to watch the Air Force Academy games located just north of the Springs. He had always wanted to be a professional player, but never made the time; his family came first. Football rubbed off on his son.

The family moved to Durango when Hammer was twelve. He played football in his younger years, in park leagues and at school, looking forward to getting bigger and faster. He loved the game and his father was his biggest fan. In high school, he was an all-state line backer and made the dean's list for academics. He wasn't extremely large at 6 feet, 200 pounds, but he loved the game. With his grades and sports abilities, Hammer was accepted to the Air Force Academy at Colorado Springs where he played tight end. His father was supremely pleased but realized that his son would never be a professional, giving way to service for his country. He was good at tight end, but not all-American. He also became infatuated with the study of flight and aeronautical engineering.

By the time Hammer graduated, an unusual growth spurt put him at 6 feet, 3 inches and 230 pounds, a little big for his goal of getting into the cockpit of a high-performance jet aircraft. The little guys usually won out for those positions, plus the competition was exhausting. It wasn't that he couldn't compete with the "best of the best" for flying jets; it was just that most of the cadets selected for jet training had come to the academy with some kind of flight training and more than the required. Most had their private pilot certificate and many had a commercial certificate or a start on one and their instrument ratings. Some had jet and turbo prop time. His family was too poor to send him for training like that. He had only been in an airplane twice.

Having been left off of the roster for fighter school and thinking of not flying at all, he was talked into the next best thing at the time. Hammer became a 0-2A Skymaster observer pilot. Military transports were not for him. He loved the smaller planes and the excitement; he was able to use his head butting football mentality while flying. The airplane wasn't that fast, but the low-level flying was a constant thrill and he became quite good at what he learned. The air force spent little time between training and then sending him to a forward base in Vietnam, where he stacked up mission after mission.

Whether using his rockets or gun pods to support ground forces, or just his flares for marking a strike, Hammer was one of the best pilots in the air force. So good, in fact, that his nickname "Hammer" stuck and he was recognized by most in the region, including the ground troops and the North Vietnamese. His first tour seemed short as he found his niche and was awarded several air medals, including one for supporting a rescue of an army commanding officer who had been shot down in a helicopter.

Hammer was sent back to the States as an instructor pilot at Peterson Field in Colorado Springs, still craving the excitement of combat and flying. Having chosen Peterson Field, since it was once his home and close to his family, the decision turned tragic when his father suddenly died, leaving a bedridden, terminally ill mother. Six months later, his mother died. Hammer was left with only a sister in some other part of the world and a duty station that he really didn't want, so he again volunteered for another tour in 'nam. Hammer's wish was granted and he looked forward to the fast and low flights over the jungle. He was always lucky in the air and his second tour lasted to the end of the conflict, which was about a year from when he returned. He received more medals and citations.

Assigned to Cannon Air Force Base in Arizona, another instructor job, he took over an idea of the commanding officers and established a program for observer pilots; much like Miramar was for jet pilots. His title was commanding officer and he held the rank of lieutenant-colonel, reporting directly to the base commander. Passionate for the flying, he created an impeccable reputation among pilots as a leader and one to work for.

During this time, Hammer met a gal named Suzanne in Albuquerque during a mutual friend's wedding. Their age difference did not seem to be a factor, with him at twenty-nine and her at twenty-two. They arranged to meet and ski at Taos and from there hit it right off. Within a year they were married. Suzanne was a nursing student, finishing her schooling that same year. During the time at Cannon, Hammer finished some schooling himself, hitting the books in the evenings and receiving a master's degree in aviation design to add to his engineering degree. Hammer was absolutely head-over-heels with Suzanne and Suzanne loved being an officer's wife.

As a result of the hard work and success of his program, Hammer was given the chance for another promotion and a station of his choice with a larger command and responsibility. The air force wanted him. However, his future was not to be in the air force and he resigned his commission to follow Suzanne to Seattle where she had dreamed of working for the emergency section of Harbor View Hospital, a nationally known medical program. Hammer took a position with a large aircraft manufacturer in Seattle and tolerated the many hours of work. He did, however, like the opportunity to work on the larger aircraft, although he never wanted to fly them. His love was still flying, but he conceded to Suzanne's wishes of being at home at least during the weekends. At this point, he was just glad to be around airplanes as an engineer and designer.

During the first five years of their life together they both worked and played hard. Both Suzanne and Hammer moved steadily up the ladder of success. During any spare time and evenings, Hammer studied for and eventually received his airframe and power plant mechanics certificate from South Seattle Voc- Tech School. A short while later he received his inspection authority. For recreation he joined a flying club on King County Field and in his spare time flew. Climbing and hiking the trails and mountains of the Cascades and Olympics, including Mount Rainier, was another passion the two shared.

He continued his flying and spent most of his time working toward a flight instructor's rating. Hammer and Suzanne both enjoyed the water and the constant activity around Seattle. But after five years together, they started to grow apart. Most of their time was spent working odd and conflicting schedules, leaving little quality time together. In 1990 and quite unexpectedly, life as they knew it changed when Jackie was born. Four years later, they were blessed with Amanda. Their life went from working all of the time to working more all of the time. It was chaotic to say the least, but no different from any other parents who sacrificed individual goals and a life of freedom for that of constant parental duties.

In 1999, a dark year, Suzanne was killed in an automobile accident and again life changed for Hammer. Having no mother, the girls needed a female role model and Sandy, Hammer's only sister, was recruited. Arrangements were made and the four moved into a house in Dillingham, Alaska. There, the opportunity arose for Hammer to buy a small air taxi company consisting of two aircraft and a hangar. At first, the girls hated the place. In fact, they hated everything. What few friends they had were left behind and they still thought about their mother.

However, Sandy was very sensitive and knowing, finding a quaint little house just west of the town with a view overlooking Nushagak Bay that made everyone forget their troubles. The trees and lowlands were green and alive with birds and grazing animals moving about wherever one looked. To the west, as far as one could see, the water changed colors as the sun or the clouds moved through. About every type of water fowl and mammal lived there. Populations of eagles, heron, king fisher, ducks, sea otters, seals and even whales could be seen during certain times. There was a road to access other areas to the west of the house, but little traffic.

Hammer couldn't stand Seattle after the loss of Suzanne. He became bitter and challenged everything. His only salvation was to get away and start anew, opening his own business in a whole different environment. Dillingham and Alaska just happened to fit what he was looking for.

Chapter 3

Sandy was a state wildlife officer, enforcing Alaskan environmental laws and protecting the native animals. With her experience as a military police officer in the army, she was a perfect candidate for a teenager's surrogate mom. Eight years younger than Hammer and having just graduated from junior college in Pueblo, she joined the army's military police unit. Like clockwork, she moved from station to station every two years throughout the world in a fifteen-year career. One day, after dreading the thought of having to deal with the Friday and Saturday late night drunks returning to base, she realized that the army was growing stale and if she was to make a life for herself it would have to be sooner rather than later. As she grew closer to her next re-up date, she kept track of positions opening for state wildlife officers. She applied for just two and within a few months was heading for the Dillingham area, the first position she opted for.

During the first six years of her army career, like her brother, she attended night classes on base and took some correspondence courses in the life sciences. She never did get a degree because she had no formal program and moving around so much. She had lots of classes and even with no degree, the Department of Wildlife was glad to have her.

She studied martial arts, having started at a very young age. She now had various degrees in several styles and would practice daily, working out with warm-ups to Tae Bo tapes and finishing with routines of Tai Chi. She could take care of herself.

Sandy had been living in a smaller house in Dillingham when Hammer called, giving her his situation. It wasn't as if they had not communicated with each other, but they lived so far away and usually only visited during the holidays. The funeral had brought them closer together the year before and since then there really had been no talk of the girls and their needs. Sandy knew that the death of Suzanne was sudden and unfortunate. Those poor little girls, she thought. Talking to Hammer, she was hesitant at first to make any commitment, but eventually agreed, also having the possibility of moving into a new house. She found enjoyment and serenity living in a larger family lifestyle. The house was perfect and the four of them, each with their own room, took little time adjusting.

Dillingham was a small town of about 2,500 people. Clouds and rain were prevalent, with a few occasionally sunny and bright, clear days thrown in. There was a lot of wind! It didn't take long for Hammer to get his business underway. With a little marketing and being one of just a few owner-operator air taxi services left in the area, he soon was delivering freight and people all over. From Nikolski to Dutch Harbor, about as far southwest as he would fly, Anchorage, Kenai, Kodiak, Cold Bay, Sand Point and between, Hammer was known for his twin-tail, twin-engine machines. He had been rejuvenated, realizing the potential of his business and the beauty of the area. People admired him for his professionalism and love of flying.

Having completely immersed himself in business and family, the time passed rapidly since he had lost his wife. He still remembered that night very well. The loss of a companion and love of a lifetime, as well as being a single parent overnight, was something he had not been ready to accept. All of the years, after the loss, had been spent putting those memories as far back in his mind as possible, right next to the memories of Vietnam. He tried to forget that night, but he was still awakened out of deep sleep many times as he felt the shutter of the car and heard the squeal of the tires just before impact. No screams, just a darkness followed by a low light as he remembered being halfway out of the passenger-side window, covered in blood. Even drenched in blood, he realized his hard head had saved him. Reaching back into the car for Suzanne, he also realized there was no hope for her. The impact was on her side and she stood no chance. The truck driver had fallen asleep and when awakened by the sounds of horns, could not react to the red light he was about to go through. Suzanne had been driving as Hammer had just closed his eyes, thinking how to spend the weekend. He was completely caught off guard, as the impact was so severe to the left side of the car that it was mostly in two pieces. Hammer received some sixty stitches throughout head and shoulders; there wasn't a piece of skin on his body without a bruise.

The year following the automobile accident, the family's lifestyle had been extremely difficult, especially without a mother for the kids. That's where Sandy had been the anchor, providing stability and with the move to Dillingham, a savior to both the girls and Hammer. He left a great suit and tie job with one of the largest companies in the United States for his start-up company in Dillingham; risky, but necessary.

Wearing a suit was the opposite attire for backcountry flying. A Pendleton shirt, a down vest and a pair of cargo pants were more his style now. Adding his military dark glasses and having the wind blowing his dark brown hair from neatness, drying his skin to wrinkles, his appearance was the epitome of toughness. He looked good and really played the part of a bush pilot.

Two opposites in lifestyle, the girls were growing up in their own directions. Attitudes were improving and now they were willing to take a chance, forgetting old memories and moving forward to meet new ones. The separation from their old school, friends, home and mother was devastating. Now, everything they knew in Seattle was fading; just a memory and remarkably, the girls liked Dillingham. The house overlooking Nushagak Bay, the wildlife and the picturesque setting was a salvation to them all. Hammer could see why Sandy loved this region.

Saturday, around noon, Hammer grabbed a handful of new charts and jumped into the truck with Francis, the girl's half standard poodle and golden retriever. They headed to the airport to pick up the magneto expected from anchorage. As planned, the plane arrived and he waited for the offloading of cargo and exchange of paper and signature. The two were then off to the hangar just a short ways away with the new mag. Francis loved to come to the airport, head out of the window with an out-of-control sloppy tongue hanging and flapping in the breeze. She knew that it would soon be exercise time.

The city had just built a biking and jogging trail near the airport that allowed Francis to run freely, sniffing all the goodies left by other animals. While Hammer replaced the magneto, she entertained herself by pushing a box of discarded and used parts around the hangar floor with her nose. She knew that eventually her turn would come as soon as Hammer finished the repair. Soon the task was finished and the ritual of putting on jogging shoes caused Francis to raise her ears and pace in frantic excitement, anticipating what was to come. Not lagging , keeping up with Hammer on the run and inhaling the fresh droppings from previous visitors was her incentive. She must have been exhausted having to stop and smell each and every scent the local dogs and wildlife left. Trying to inhale all of those pungent aromas and then trying to catch up to Hammer's pace was pure dog heaven. For Francis, this was what she lived for.

When Hammer got back to the hangar, out of breath, he tried another call to Bill. There was no answer. Hammer hated an empty airplane and knew Bill would need supplies. No cargo meant he would have to pay for the fuel.

Sunday came, Hammer having replaced the magneto the previous day and having had an enjoyable Saturday evening with the girls. An earlier phone call announced that the freight would be ready and early at the outer most taxi area on the airport for Hammer to pick up. A Panel truck stating "A. Lawton Construction Company" on the side panel waited. 78 Bravo taxied to the truck where there were twenty-four boxes of dynamite to be loaded and tied down to the seat tracks. There was a cargo net that would do just the trick for more support for the boxes. Hammer was planning a late departure, but with the freight early, was airborne two hours before schedule. 78B was at King Salmon by noon and with the help of the receiving company, the dynamite was off loaded to their truck in a few minutes. His clients loved it when their freight was early, especially on a Sunday. Hammer topped off the wing tanks and then decided to head northeast to Iliamna to see if Bill was okay. It was a last-minute decision, but he had to know.

The flight took little time from King Salmon, with favorable winds enabling a good ground speed. Overflying the lodge at about a thousand feet was just for observation and habit, trying to get radio contact. He had no luck with the radio. Hammer noticed that the men on the perimeter, surrounding the lodge, were still in place. He made a sharp bank to the left and dropped down to a few hundred feet above the ground, overflying the lodge about a hundred yards to the north. At a speed of 150 knots and a couple of hundred feet off the deck, the lodge and buildings swooshed by.

"What was that?" Hammer said to himself. It was kind of a light tapping sound. He hoped he had everything tied down in back or he had not left a shroud dangling out of the door. It wasn't noticeable until now; just after that tight turn inbound. Checking gauges, everything seemed okay, but the left aileron and rudder had a different feel. Something had happened on the fly-by.

An abandoned gravel strip just up the way was left by an oil expedition company years ago. It would do just the trick. He wasn't about to turn sharply back to Bill's strip and he was more than half way to the other strip anyway. Hammer landed and taxied to the end, shutting the engines down and hopping out. He thought he knew exactly what the problem would be. That jolt of turbulence just before land at the end of the lake must have loosened something.

He was certainly wrong on that thought. He couldn't believe what he was seeing. There were bullet holes in his airplane. Not many, but enough to make flying feel different and enough to tick him off. Where did they come from? Then he told himself, "Don't be stupid. Something's going on at Bill's." With this proof, he could not deny that Bill needed his help. He certainly wasn't expecting bullets, but there was no mistaking what he saw.

There were holes in the left aileron and the tail section, with one hole going up through the fin. He was in shock with the old times now in front of him. He had been lucky again. The bullets had missed the engines and fuel cells. The closer he examined, the more holes were revealed and they hadn't missed by much. There was one hole two feet behind the pilot seat that had ricocheted off the left wheel. The tire was now flat. The landing and weight of the plane was enough to cause a leak from a deep groove in the tire. He was in the middle of nowhere with a shot up airplane. All he needed now was a sniper shooting at him to be back in 'nam.

CHAPTER 4

Anchorage was continuously dark and dreary, under a rainy overcast sky as Mark had just finished organizing the stacks of handwritten profiles and tattered field documents the teams had submitted to him after their investigations. The results of their probes and fact finding efforts needed to be entered in the computer and backed up on disks. Some names were mentioned and some photos were submitted, but there was no real connection to any particular person, company, freight handler or method of transportation. He figured that in Anchorage, being of medium size and having only one logical way of transportation—the sea—it should be easy to track movements of containers. The way of transporting by land would have the trucks cross several borders and smugglers usually did not want any part of that. If the cargo was coming in, the FBI had the equipment for observing movement. Containers came in from as far south as Los Angeles and it would be simple to track the comparatively few funneling in to the city. Due to the sheer quantity and thinking about the number of team members, a task of this magnitude might be more than his small unit could handle. He needed the impossible—more people and equipment to cover the containers. If not, they would be blind and hit or miss to intercept any contraband.

Reports of illegal arms and equipment being shipped and submitted by the local law enforcement, the state troopers and even military sources were of no value. In his "in" box Mark had seen only four such reports and two had been there for a couple of years. Wondering how come no one took the information seriously, he tried to rationalize why no one cared, why the infiltration of a possible al-Qaeda cell was unimportant. This state was perfect for cell infiltration. Maybe his team was so naïve to think that a cell could never infiltrate a state like Alaska, but after all, New York had paid the ultimate price in 9-11.

Mark had met with his boss that morning and was advised to be on the alert to excessive expenses. "Already!" he exclaimed while grinding his teeth in frustration. He knew that he would be cut off for the funding he needed, but so soon? He was desperate for information, not a shorter leash. He was told to get approval on any operation through normal channels before proceeding. Now it was obvious what that snide, snickering attitude earlier on had meant. His boss was in on his imminent failure, probably requested by the upper echelon. Mark would have no part of failure. At the present, he would fudge on those decisions to get approval. If he wasn't given a fair chance he knew he would fail. At this point he would let his teams continue for the rest of the week before giving them the budget news. Maybe they could still come up with some significant information. He was not going to fail again.

Hammer figured he was about six and a half to seven miles northwest of the lodge. He also knew that the plane had to be ready to fly before he went anywhere. Patching the holes and making sure the thin skin would not tear, being physically ready for flight, was his first priority. He was a veteran at fixing holes and with a roll of heavy duty duct tape from his tool bag proceeded to cut two-inch round patches to place over the voids in the aluminum. The holes, guessing to be from 7.62 mm bullets, had sharp edges protruding away from the entry side that needed to be pushed back in and then covered with a round patch of tape. If accessible, both sides were patched.

Using a simple screw jack he carried in the plane, Hammer lifted the left axle and landing strut high enough to remove the wheel. Snipping the safety wire from the bolt heads holding the inboard brake pads, he removed the bolts and disassembled the brakes. Cutting the cotter pin and unscrewing the nut that held the wheel to the axle, he took the parts completely loose and proceeded to unbolt the wheel halves to remove the tire and tube. As soon as everything was apart, he put a patch over the hole in the inner tube and another inside the tire. With the wheel assembled again, he pumped the tire back up to forty-five PSI with his hand pump and then put the wheel back on the axle, tightening the axle nut. Backing off the nut slightly to gain alignment to the hole for the pin, he installed a new cotter pin from his bag. The brakes were put back together and tightened. He finished by installing new safety wire.

There was one fortunate thought: the engines were not damaged. He finished the repairs and with a sigh he thought, "I expected this type of crap in Vietnam, but not out here." Firing up the front engine, 78 Bravo was repositioned so the plane was ready for an immediate take-off. Hammer shut down the engine, checked fuel, checked oil levels and covered as much of the airplane as he could with a camouflaged tarp from the cargo compartment. He didn't expect to hide the whole plane, just break up the lines, making it less visible.

Hammer thought that he would never be in a position like the one he was in now. Vietnam, and the dangers it held, was so long ago. The hair on the back of his neck was standing straight out with adrenaline and hostility; he was irritated, to say the least. He also grew more concerned about Bill. He knew the best thing to do would be to head for King Salmon and the military, but Bill was mostly on his mind. He would take that eight-mile hike to see what was going on at the lodge and then find help.

Most pilots in Alaska carried survival equipment in their planes. Hammer was no different and now he would have to rely on those items he had. He emptied the contents of the plane's survival pack and he selected water bottles, a VHF hand radio, granola bars, binoculars, a flashlight, a length of rope, and a small first aid kit. He wrapped the remaining food back up in the original bag and taped it shut. Bears could easily destroy a plane looking for food just from the slightest scent. His cell phone was completely useless out here and he normally didn't carry a satellite phone.

Hammer stuffed all of the items, plus a utility tool, back in the pack. He grabbed his Marlin .45-70 guide gun, taking it out of the protective case and leaning it against the plane. He stuffed the only box of ammunition into one of his vest pockets and a compass and chart in a different pocket. Then he slipped the pack over his shoulders, shut the doors of the plane and grabbed the rifle, and walked to the end of the runway closest to the lake.

Now at three in the afternoon, he estimated he could make the lodge in a few hours with some luck. He was anxious to start moving as he withdrew the compass and identified a tree in the distance to use as a reference for direction. He would walk to that tree and then take another bearing, using another landmark. The lake was on his left and it would keep him from getting lost as long as he kept it in sight. A little voice in his subconscious said, "So you're a tough guy?" He thought for a moment and replied honestly, "I should hope so because I don't know what's out there or what I'm getting myself into!" Another moment passed and he said aloud, "This is a crazy idea. Where can I get help?" His mind raced to the realization that there would be *no* help.

Little did he know that his decision to find his friend and to offer whatever help he could, if needed, would be the beginning of a gigantic life-altering experience. He needed more information about whoever shot at him. He wanted that chance to get even with the hole punchers. Should he continue or call in the law? Hammer was no coward and he had a responsibility to his friend. His conclusion was from thought and circumstance; he *was* a tough guy and would see this through.

There were not a lot of tall trees, just short, thick scrub brush around this area of the lake; the vegetation was kept low from the consistently high winds. To the north the trees were abundant and mostly evergreen. A few taller trees were scattered around the south side. At somewhere near a thousand yards out from the air strip and on line with his sight tree, Hammer looked back to where the airplane was parked. It stood out like a seven-foot center on a basketball team of munchkins. Hopefully, with the advent of night, the airplane would blend well enough with the surroundings to remain hidden.

The walking conditions were not difficult at first, and he mostly followed animal trails, keeping an eye out for dangerous animals. The area was packed with small game trails. The country was full of moose and deer tracks. A few signs of black bear were present. Some of the mixed tracks were probably caribou.

Despite tripping and stumbling over small rocks that were occasionally hidden on the ground and thinking that they were placed there just to twist his ankles by Mother Nature, Hammer grew tiresome and easily irritated from the constant tripping, but kept up a good walking pace for the first three miles. A pedometer would have come in handy to estimate distances. He made a mental note to put one in his pack when he got back, as if he would be doing this again. With the brush increasing in depth and density, something was always trying to snag his legs and feet from the crotch down; he estimated his walking speed had dropped to about two miles per hour and would only be getting worse as he moved from the lowlands to the steeper hills.

The underbrush was certainly not like walking on a sidewalk. It was supported by uneven wet dirt and high saw-tooth grass concealing an occasional softball-sized rock. Clothing would not last long moving through the undergrowth, being penetrated and clawed at by the extensions of branches tearing at whatever moved by. On the trails, tuffs of fur could be spotted regularly, having been pulled from animals using the same path.

At five miles out from the strip, the terrain started to vary with a gradual rise and the shoreline of the lake difficult to see through the denser and taller brush. Hammer was confused by the lack of wildlife, but with the noise he was making, the animals were probably frightened off. If the animals were hesitant about being seen, maybe he should have been too! Hammer could sense something or someone was near, the hair on the back of his neck was straight out again.

Mostly thinking of the lodge setting and what he might find, Hammer's concerns were with Bill. *What is Bill's situation?* Knowing there were armed men surrounding the lodge with attitudes to put holes in planes, possibly causing the aircraft to crash, he wondered how he would handle the situation alone. Thinking of different tactics, he realized the uselessness of guessing at this point. The best bet would be to wait and see what he would find and not fantasize about different scenarios. His main focus should now be on the trail and not being detected, making sure he could get back out. He also thought of his buddies from the service or even his sister and how great it would be to have them along for back up. Too late now!

"Snap out of it! Pay attention to what's going on," he said to himself. "Find the facts and assess the situation." Walking so far in the tundra was not what he was prepared for. His emotions were wandering in all directions and causing lightheadedness.

He paused for a much needed drink and a short rest. Too much rest and he would stiffen. Hammer was realizing that he was a pilot and not trained as a grunt. Those early PT sessions had been long gone and his physical condition was not the same as that of an active young military man.

Some relief came from the rest and water. Hammer took in landmarks and the surroundings; he judged the time and amount of light left before nightfall as he sat below a small outcropping of rocks. Even in these circumstances, this was a beautiful place with all of Mother Nature's colors. He kept himself from lulling to lethargy by looking at his watch, judging by the sun when it might get dark and some kind of logical means of determining the remaining distance. Hammer's hopes were to remain alert as he lifted his progressively heavier and heavier body to his feet to continue his slow pace, looking for any movement or hearing any noise around him.

The overcast was thin and not threatening rain and the wind was about ten knots, a good steady light breeze whistling by his ears. The wind made for a good means to hide the sounds of his walking. He knew that the lodge was close and he took his time. No need to be spotted first and then be the hunted. He didn't know the true identity of the enemy yet. With binoculars, he scanned the area, noting the abundance of plant life; the low-lying brush grew in every direction. He knew he was close; the hair on the back of his neck was twitching even more, causing him to be at his peak awareness. He moved slowly and carefully, one well-placed step at a time. After a few steps he would stop to observe anything that indicated the presence of another human.

Ever so slight, a new sound began making its way to his senses, faintly and then loudly. The gusts of wind were altering the volume of music he heard making it audible one moment and silent the next. Along with the music, the hum of a generator was getting louder. He still could not see the lodge, but he knew he was in the danger zone now.

CHAPTER 5

Barely visible in the distance, the lodge seemed different. Maybe it was the sentries stationed around the outside or possibly the loud music coming from the inside. He could smell the curry and spices of a different style of food cooking, much different from the scent of barbeque. He could also hear loud laughter above unidentifiable language from the guests. Hammer took a few items from his pack and then placed it behind a clump of dead grass, covering it with some branches from the ground. He also had his radio, a small pair of binoculars, a flashlight, and the utility tool. In his larger pockets he carried a couple of bottles of water and a few granola bars. He made sure the .45-70 was fully loaded.

The men were still in place around the lodge and he was not sure he wanted to tangle with what appeared to be automatic weapons they all carried. Watching their movements and slowly getting closer, he moved to an observation point as close as he dared. Having been in combat and developing that sixth sense, even while flying, Hammer was feeling he was in over his head. At least his neck hair wasn't sticking straight out; it lay flat on his neck, washed by sweat.

There was something different besides the strange noise and smells that caught his eye. Wires! He had been watching every step and it paid off. He wondered where they went and what they were for. Backtracking quietly several yards from his forward position, he moved out of sight of the guards, following the wound pair of wires. What he found was unbelievable. *Why would anyone place claymore mines out here? Who are these guys?* He had carried crates of these mines to the front in Vietnam, but pilots didn't usually deal with the business end of the devices. He took a dead branch from the ground and peeled off the smaller twigs, thrusting the thick end in the dirt with as much might as he dared, keeping as quiet as possible and thinking that marking the mine would help for a speedy retreat.

Hammer was starting to get a different type of adrenaline rush. *What have I gotten myself into?* Observing the situation and analyzing the strength of the opposing force from his camouflaged position was something he hadn't thought he would ever be doing. He looked at the arrangement of guards. He might be out of his league on this venture, but what about Bill? Thoughts of how to handle the situation were not generating in his mind. Answers had to come quickly or he would head back to the airplane. Military people will agree that their training in the service, especially in combat, is never forgotten. The training was for the welfare of the soldiers as they worked in teams. However, too many years had gone by since he had been in the face of any enemy. He was young and cocky then, and not a mature and somewhat hesitant adult!

His emotions were difficult to control, with one side wanting to charge in and the other wanting to go for help. His only hope was that he would respond quickly to any situation if one arose, regardless of the lack of practice or preparation.

He moved in as close as he dared, hiding in the tall grass and bushes, hoping the light brown and greens of his shirt and vest would blend in with the environment and not give him away. He tucked tufts of grass in his clothing wherever he could. His face was covered by sweat and he wiped loose dirt on his cheeks and forehead.

He found an even closer place for observation. The low grass and branches camouflaged his outline, and he was careful not to reflect any type of light or make fast movements. Another hour went by.

During that time he found out just what he wanted. The guards, a group of slender dark complexioned men dressed in mostly white, would rotate between designated posts every half hour. These men were professional, not getting stale in one spot and always being alert when they moved. They would not be predictable. He was hoping that the number of guards would somehow reduce, but they never gave any indications of doing so. There were a total of eight guards at one time. He could only see three in his scan and assumed the others were around the other side of the lodge. The odds were at least eight to one and undoubtedly much larger with the guards inside; all of the men had automatic weapons. There was no indication of the goings-on inside, their activity was a mystery. Hammer kept eyeing the strip to the southeast. *How did they get here? The runway was adequate for a plane like the Skymaster and maybe a Navajo, but not big enough for a plane to haul all of these guys and their equipment. Where is their transportation?* With the lodge runway barely visible at a quarter mile away, there was no sign of an airplane.

He didn't know whether it was dumb luck or just timing, but the question of transportation was answered almost as soon as the thought had come to mind. The distinctive beating of rotors, the percussive waves of the blades slicing through the air, getting closer and louder, indicated an inbound helicopter. The sound soon revealed a large, dark machine descending down to the front yard of the lodge and landing. There were no distinctive marks or numbers on the outside to indicate where it was from. After landing, four men departed the chopper and were greeted by a group of eight from the lodge. The whine of the turbines and spinning of the non-lifting blades disguised the voices as the men moved up the stairs to the outside deck of the lodge. The chopper would probably soon lift off since the pilot kept the blades rotating and the turbines at a low whine.

Tony Larucci and his entourage were greeted by his son at the helicopter pad and escorted through the large cathedral-style doors at the entrance to the lodge. Tony was glad they had chosen Alaska for their operation and had codenamed it, suitably, *Caribou.* Their cell had planned to place high explosives on several sections of the oil pipeline and several pumping stations, disrupting flow and causing chaos. At the same time, another group of cell members would hit several major canneries and ships up and down the peninsula and the panhandle. To complete the operation they would cause chaos on the military bases with high explosives, placing them in strategic locations for optimal damage. The idea was not strictly destruction, but that terrorism could strike at any time and any place on the infidels' own sacred ground. Very much like 9/11, with the satisfaction of destruction and loss of infidel life, chaos and mayhem would be brought to the infidels on their own land without a means of protection. No one could protect the sparsely populated Alaskans. One had to have an easy target to start with, and Alaska was, quite frankly, too easy!

Named Assad Multah Mohamad by his mother, Tony was the worst of the worst of a human form. He was orphaned in Saudi Arabia at an early age and hung around the riffraff of the drug and gun smugglers to help make money and scrounge food to survive. At age fourteen, he loved to shoot and show the older resistance members that he was as good as they were at killing and belonged with them. Even at this young age he had killed many. At twenty-two and a trained terrorist and infidel hater, he received a visa for school in California, attending Stanford. Tony was smart and deceptive, graduating and receiving a diploma for business administration. He established a company in the Los Angeles area dealing with shipping and merchandise using money supplied by his fellow al-Qaeda brothers oversees for transporting illegal contraband. During the late eighties he helped any militant organization, working as a sponsor, shipping explosives and arms into the United States.

The need for an al-Qaeda operative in Alaska was of interest to him and the more he found out about the state, the more he thought it would be gravy. Throughout his business dealings he was unafraid to break any law, whether it was governmental or humanitarian. If he wanted something, he would take it or destroy it. The same went for his hired help or his acquaintances. His henchmen were becoming well-known among the head al-Qaeda throughout the world, completing any task and performing the most ghoulish and profane killings. Nothing was too low for Tony.

Tony relinquished his company in mid-2001. The Los Angeles holdings went to another top member and Tony established a new company, Alaskan Machine and Supply, a front for the al-Qaeda in Anchorage, Alaska. He ran supplies, drugs, and arms through his small warehouse on the east side of Anchorage. Tony did not particularly want to deal with the drug market because of the number of buyers and dealers involved. It was just too much work and more visibility for getting caught. Drugs were also messy, but they caused a need for the low life and consequently distressed the general population by increasing theft and homicide. He found this was a cheap way to disrupt the infidels by increasing the need for law enforcement, causing taxes and disharmony. As any good businessman does, the company grew larger and larger. He purchased two oceangoing freighters and a small fleet of cargo planes. With these he was able to provide drugs and equipment, and any other illegal product, to anyone who desired it. Things were going well and now all he needed were teams to carry out mission Caribou.

Darby Rivers was the second in command in Toni's company. Rivers had one thing in mind: getting back at the people who killed his family. Younger than Toni, Darby was trained in the al-Qaeda camps in Afghanistan. He too was sent to the United States with a student visa to get an education and then raise havoc with the infidels. Darby's brother Charles, known as Chuck, headed one of the operations and loved the ability to do whatever he wanted. With unlimited funds and a lack of respect toward anyone except his comrades, Chuck would take what he wanted or just take and cut a throat. Witnesses were shot, resisters were beaten and he, with no limits or conscience, just didn't care. He knew he could get the better of anyone or any situation; he had no rules to play by. Darby ran most of the operations for the Larucci Co. and Chuck dealt with the security. The three of them plus a half-dozen top men from the lower forty eight, along with their henchmen, now enjoyed the hospitality at the lodge.

Hammer knew he was out numbered and outmuscled. The nearest help was in King Salmon at the military base. He didn't even know if they had ground enough troops to handle these guys. They were mostly air support. *How can I alert them?* Hammer reached for his two-way radio, but the radio was no use. It was just for aircraft and line of sight. He was buried between hills and a long ways away. He might be able to reach a Japan Airlines jet outbound from Anchorage, but that would be stretching the range on the low-powered handheld. He had plenty of time to think of a plan since the daylight was almost gone.

At first, the darkness would be on Hammer's side. With the discovery of claymores, he would be limited to where he could move around; unadvisable to move at all would be more to the point. The brush was thick and full of stickers. He didn't dare use the flashlight. He kept scanning the outline of one particular building, about a hundred feet to the northwest. One thing was for sure: something or someone was in the out building; there was a guard at the door. Judging by the looks of the automatic weapon the guard held, they didn't want something or someone in, or out. Hammer decided to move closer to the building since it would take little effort and he had good cover. They hadn't been changing the guard on the shed and he figured that one of them against one of him would be the best odds. The helicopter was not going to be a diversion after all. The pilot had shut the turbines down, probably just waiting for them to cool at low RPMs. The guests had moved into the lodge and it was Hammer's turn, moving ever so slowly through the low underbrush, making his way to a position near the side of the out building. The side he chose was opposite the guard and he would be out of sight of the lodge.

By now the natural light was about used up. The helicopter had been shut down, so his initial assumption was wrong. It would probably be there for the night. The distant generator hum still covered any noise that he made, working around the sides of the small building. On the way to the building, he noticed two more pairs of twisted wires, having almost tripped on both. He marked them as he had before and made a mental map of their location for his retreat.

The guards continued rotating shifts every half hour, carrying their ominous flat black-and-wood-colored weapons wherever they went. That kept any notion of reconnoitering the lodge away. Hammer made no mistake identifying the older AK 47s—he had seen so many of in 'nam. He also saw no way to combat them. There were a few newer models he wasn't familiar with, but most had Kalashnikovs. They all wore Kevlar combat vests with pockets full of magazines and grenades fastened to clips hanging from the front or in small pockets in the front. One thing for sure: he knew he would have to go back to the plane much faster than he had come in. His only advantage to this point would be the darkness of night along with his knowledge of the terrain and the route back to the tiny strip. The few twenty-foot trees close to the lodge made the only cover; the rest of the vegetation had been flattened or destroyed.

Hammer knew these guys didn't expect any unwanted visitors. They were too lax. What about Bill? Bill was about Hammer's age, but had a build like a grizzly. In fact, that was probably why he never had bear problems. They must have thought he was one of them. Hammer chuckled at the thought of his friend and the image he created. It was mostly from nerves.

Hammer counted the number of sentries and other men in or around the lodge that he could see from his vantage point behind the small building. He was much closer now. He had some crazy thoughts about being aggressive, but just seeing how many automatic weapons they had changed any thought he might have had. He needed a diversion. In the diminishing light, he would stick with his original plan to use the sound of the helicopter to disguise what movements he made. His only problem was when the chopper would leave. If the chopper didn't leave, the most time he could spend was an hour before daylight, and at that time he would make his way back to the plane.

He thought about what different tactics he might use without exposing himself and getting caught or even worse, doing something stupid and getting shot. A quarter moon was rising and the light would help for a retreat. The breaks in the clouds would allow for cover and to help with a fast backtrack. The helicopter just sat with its droopy blades and no pilot in sight.

The more he sat, the more he was sure that he should head to the plane and get help. The odds were against him here, and he had no information about Bill. By the looks of these men, Bill still might be alive, but not likely. The gamble to make a move, whenever that might be, would have to go exactly his way. There was just too much against him and too many variables.

Hammer started to move back to the brush from the cover of the small building, resigning to the fact that he couldn't handle the situation alone, when he heard a groan. He froze. He was on the side of the small building that was not only hidden from the lodge, but just opposite the generator and its hum. There it was again, more of a growl than a mown. *Is it the guards talking? Is it Bill?* Hammer changed his thinking. He would lay low and wait until the guards moved to their new positions. The more he moved the more chance of his discovery by the guards. If he had a chance, he would take out the guard and check to see if anybody was in the shed. If there was nothing, he would *di di mau* to the lodge later and get back to the plane to call for help. One other option was a small window on the back side of the shed.

CHAPTER 6

At a low crawl, Hammer moved along the back of the building. He hesitated for a minute, checking for more guards, when he heard the distinctive sounds of turbines starting and building RPMs. He couldn't believe his luck! The distraction of the chopper starting was just the opportunity he was waiting for. The sound level increased as he moved to the shed and examined the small window. In the open now, there was no brush to hide his movements or his silhouette.

At first glance, it was obvious that he could not fit through the opening of the window. With the help of the blade on his utility tool and the loud noise of the spinning blades and turbines of the helicopter, he began to chip away at the wood. Covered by years of dirt and moss, he could not see through the window. Hammer took a quick peek at the lodge. About ten men, well dressed and appearing to be the leaders, mostly carrying drinks and not guns were standing, talking to each other, waiting for the signal to board the chopper. Their definition was hampered by having to look through debris being kicked up by the chopper blades and the waves of hot air spewing from the exhaust. The guards were all watching, as the small group talked and laughed, moving toward the dark machine as it came to life.

Hammer worked like a mad man with his small hand tool, quickly making progress on the rotting wood. Chunks of wood flew off into the nearby brush, the impact disguised by the helicopter.

Finally he was able to pry the window open, barely enough to get his head through the opening. He had more work to do and again attacked the wood frame. With a little extra effort whittling, the window frame soon gave way, enabling him to slide his head and a single shoulder through the opening. Scanning the inside of the building with his flashlight, he was able to identify mostly shelving filled with stores and canned goods, with a few piles of junk in the corners; five skinned carcasses of caribou and deer hung from the rafters. Suddenly, the entire area was ablaze with light. The pilot had activated his landing lights for the passengers to load. Hammer was fortunate to be away from the light. He was half in and half out of the tiny hole. All it would take was a curious guard to venture around the building to ruin his day.

The helicopter left quickly as Hammer held his breath in anticipation of a guard appearing. It never happened, and he went back to his business of searching the shed with his light, using the distraction of the departing chopper. All was what he expected for a storage shed, except in the far corner, there was a neatly wrapped and tied bundle. It was Bill. His eyes were partially open in the presence of Hammer's light, with a noticeable trail of dried blood that had dribbled down his face and on his shirt. Hammer gave him the quiet sign and thumbs-up. Hammer knew what he had to do.

Bill was a bit of a whale now, but Hammer knew Bill could still take care of himself. When they had met, Hammer was the pilot for one of Bill's fishing trips. They became friends right off, both being ex-military. Bill had been army and was very appreciative of the air force's efforts supporting their ground activities in 'nam.

From a poor family living in the southern United States, he moved regularly to wherever his mother could find work. More dysfunctional than any other description, the family settled in Oklahoma, where his divorced mother married an oilrig mechanic. They rented a two-bedroom house near Tulsa.

Bill only had one desire at the time: to be a successful entrepreneur and open some kind of business. He saw the painful efforts his mother spent to put food on the table, always having to work long hours.

He also had friends with families who had everything. Knowing what being poor was like, he knew he could help his family and his mother especially. At ten, he started his own business of delivering papers, catalogs, and anything else. His business grew steadily and in a short four months went from a one-person operation to having three neighborhood boys working for him. At twelve he had saved most of his earnings that were not needed for the family and with some advice from his stepfather, invested in the more secure stocks, learning at an early age about finances.

Bill became a football maniac. All through junior high and high school he loved playing the game. He was an all-star linebacker for the local community college. Football was what kept him in school because his interest in the schoolwork surely didn't. Bill dropped out after the second football season was over. It wasn't that Bill was dumb. He just had different ideas about school and the required work. He spent most of his time thinking of the perfect business and what he would do with unlimited money. His dreams were cut short by the draft and away he went to Fort Lewis in Washington for basic training and then AIT. Bill found something he was really good at and was sent to Fort Carson, Colorado to ranger school. Vietnam was almost immediate after graduation and he spent his first four years in and out of harm's way, volunteering year after year for in-country service. His training and experience gave him a specialty the army needed and he was the best at it. It was special ops and top secret.

Bill, having completed four years in 'nam, was sent back to Fort Bragg as an instructor. The Pentagon offered him several different posts, but he settled on Bragg. As a noncommissioned officer, he was not shown the respect he thought he should have been given for the work he did. He was disenchanted with the cadre and again volunteered for 'nam. Sent back, not in his old MOS but as a noncom platoon leader, he finished his tour as the Vietnam conflict came to an end. He then went to Fort Lewis again and was given the opportunity to stay in the army with bonuses and E-8 stripes, but he declined after some comment by a non combat officer that ticked him off.

Bill headed back to the local community college, trying to increase his knowledge of current business practices. He always kept in contact with his mother and did what he could to help her and what was left of his family. In the next ten years, with only his associate's degree, he spent his time roaming around the western states taking any job available to supply the juice for his dreams, Jack Daniels and a warm and dry place to sleep.

In 1990 Bill caught a break, a big one at that. In the previous ten years, he had kept track of his mother, stepfather, and family, but time had passed so rapidly in his state of inebriation that he lost all reality of much of that time. His mother had died in a traffic accident, and in her will she had left him most everything. The other members of the family were all gone; his stepfather had died, and of his two brothers, one had died in 'nam and the other was nowhere to be found.

Included in the will was a brand new Mercedes, a replacement from the insurance company for the one that was wrecked; the house, old but in a prime real-estate area; and, finally, a good deal of money. His mother, like Bill, saved every penny and her husband had been a working fool, starting out as an oilrig mechanic and working his way to the top, becoming a company board member.

Bill was quite rich now and decided to get professional help with his drinking problem. He wanted to dry out and get a good start on a new business venture. In a few months, he was a new Bill. He was driven and became savvy to the current market and its values. Daily he would monitor his resources, investing in the Russell 2000 and he followed stock in the New York Stock exchange and the NASDAQ. In a few years he made his first purchase: a pair of restaurants in Seattle. Although hesitant to spend so much money, he saw a great opportunity and in time doubled his investment.

He decided to build and open a third restaurant in the south Lake Union area. Before the third building was open, he was offered a purchase price for his company he couldn't refuse. His dream of owning a business was displaced by dollar signs. The deal was finalized, check was received and he was again left with no business. He was much richer, mind you, but not an owner. He burnt himself out on this last project so he took a two-week vacation, as he did every year, spending time fishing in Alaska.

It was during these trips that Hammer and Bill met. Bringing supplies in and taking people back and forth to their camps,

Hammer would regularly cross paths with Bill. Hammer eventually invited Bill to stay at his house when he was not in the bush. Bill loved this life, totally opposite of the high-paced Seattle life. When the lodge at Lake Iliamna came up for sale, Bill didn't even blink at the offer, paying cash for the buildings and property.

Bill and Hammer flew over the lake and landed at the strip nearby, getting a bird's eye view that was most spectacular. The lodge needed work, but all Bill could see was another dream come true. Bill proceeded to improve the building and advertise great food and relaxation. He soon had his own fishing guide license, with help from Hammer. He hired Hammer to be the exclusive carrier, responsible for the transportation of his clients. A world-class cook was hired to bolster the "five star restaurant." The business was on its way to success with his reputation from Seattle and was being booked for months in advance. At the end of the first year, the lodge was so busy that he quit trying to get customers, having booked for two years in advance. He just kicked back and enjoyed what he had, not wanting to burn out again.

As the chopper continued to lift and fly away from the compound, Hammer quickly moved from his position, straight to the front of the shed. Everyone's attention was focused on the departing noise and blinking lights. This was exactly what Hammer needed as he made a quick glance around the corner of the shed. The guard was surprised only for a split second before a rifle butt whacked him on the side of the head. There was no moan, just the sound of a thump that was covered by the chopper and generator. Hammer pulled the unconscious guard to the side, out of sight.

The larger group of men had moved back in to the lodge, the noise from their voices diminishing, as was the chopper. Hammer checked the door on the shed, and there was no lock, just a latch that was easily opened. He released the latch, slid through a small slit between door and jamb, closing the door quickly for cover. Shining his light around the inside until he found Bill, he moved directly to the corner, untying his friend and helping him to his unsteady feet.

Bill was glad to see Hammer, and by this time, he was ready to take on the whole bunch of terrorists. Hammer let him know what he had seen and heard. The mines were one of Hammer's only concerns for a hasty retreat, as he explained to Bill what the situation was. Bill casually told him "No worries."

Hammer and Bill talked about a plan over a few sips of water and they agreed that the best action was to head to the plane and get help. Perching the unconscious guard by the door in a position like he was doing his job, they backtracked the way Hammer had come, slowly and stealthily. They could see objects, but not very clearly in the dark. The moon was some help when out of the clouds as Hammer pointed out the wires he had marked. Bill did his thing, disabling and hiding them. He said in his gruff dry voice, "This is pretty old stuff. The new models are wireless." He also found a few mines Hammer had missed.

The hike back seemed to take forever and Bill lost whatever sharpness and stamina he had. *They must have pounded on him for a long time,* Hammer surmised as he occasionally looked back to his friend. They didn't talk until it was time to stop and rest.

The two rested a short time and knew that sooner or later the guards would discover the unconscious man propped against the building. They rested only long enough for a few sips of water from the bottles in Hammer's pack, having retrieved it from the hiding spot. Bill climbed to his feet and continued walking, giving no excuses, even in the obvious pain he was in. The walk out was much more difficult than the walk in. They had little visibility and everything they went by, from branches to grass to rocks, grabbed at their clothes and skin, causing them to slip or trip or be cut to the meat. They agreed that the bad guys couldn't find them in the dark without dogs and they didn't hear any.

It was tough going, but the lake edge, meadow, and then the small landing strip appeared directly in front of them. Between a jog, limp, and drag, Bill and Hammer made the length of the strip, pulled the tarp off and climbed into the plane, tossing the equipment in back.

Hammer started the plane and, with no runway lights, took a bearing from his directional gyro directly down what appeared to be the center of the runway. There was no marked centerline! He added power, turned on the landing lights, and they were soon off the ground with a short field takeoff, airborne for King Salmon and the closest hospital for Bill. Law enforcement was lean in the small towns on the peninsula, so the best bet was the military.

As soon as they were airborne, Hammer shut off all of the exterior lights until they were out of the area. Those bad guys, whoever they were, were highly armed and both Hammer and Bill wanted no part of them, at least with the equipment they had at hand. As soon as 78 Bravo had sufficient altitude, Hammer called King Salmon flight service and told them their arrival time and to alert the MPs and the hospital. Circling the short gravel strip after takeoff, the light of a half moon was not bright enough to conceal a number of small lights in a row, about two miles out from the strip. Besides the lights, they could also see muzzle flashes from weapons. These guys, whoever they were, had tracked the two at night in difficult terrain. They were either good or lucky.

Both Hammer and Bill knew they were lucky to just get out of that fix alive. The two in the plane eventually made their way to King Salmon in the partial moonlit dark of night, Hammer wondering the whole trip if there would be more holes to patch.

CHAPTER 7

The trip to King Salmon didn't seem long, but Bill was in pain and curled up in the right seat like a dog licking his wounds. The ambulance was waiting to escort him to the hospital after they landed. He was worse off than Hammer had thought, with a broken nose, some broken ribs, a few teeth missing, and several dislocated fingers he had put back in place by himself. Internally he was a mess. They couldn't tell what was damaged until tests had been done.

Hammer called Sandy to let her know where he was and that he and Bill would head back when they were through at the base. After the doctors had finished with Bill, he declined the hospital and joined Hammer in the mess hall to snack on anything they could find and take advantage of some of that fine military coffee. It turned out to be better than he had remembered. The local law enforcement, some high-ranking officers of the MPs and a state patrol officer temporarily stationed in King Salmon had arrived to find out exactly what all of the commotion was about. The base commander had alerted them, as well as the FBI in Anchorage. The MPs set up a conference room in a building across from the mess hall and the entire conglomeration of men gathered around a table.

Hammer sat back, coffee in hand, listening while Bill made an effort to explain what had happened as well as he could. Although at times he was difficult to understand, Bill described a story that sounded like a thriller from Hollywood. He told of how a group of men looking like any normal well dressed business men, had booked his entire lodge for two weeks and as soon as they had arrived had taken over with strong arm tactics and firearms. They tied him up and tossed him into the small building when he refused to cooperate. When the plane brought supplies, they wanted him to reply on the radio, but he wouldn't. That was his first beating. Eventually, they got three words out of him on a recorder for a reply. In and out of consciousness, he was about to give up any hope at all of being rescued when he noticed a bright light in his face. That's when Hammer appeared.

The first fifteen men at the lodge were soon accompanied by another thirty for support and security. Bill filled in the smallest of details and observations and was exceptionally thorough. One fact was missing. He was not sure about any motive for the men being there.

Bill wasn't even sure what language they spoke. It was definitely an Eastern language. He said he would be willing to go back to the lodge after them, now! When Bill was through, it was Hammer's turn to add his two bits worth. He really didn't have much to add, other than what he saw. He told of the fly over and the holes in his plane. He described the helicopter and the mines. Hammer hesitated as he watched Bill tilt in his chair, realizing that Bill had had enough. He looked at the general and mentioned that he and Bill were both tired and said that if there was someplace to eat nearby; they would both like to "have a bite and then get some sack time." The general was more than generous and said he would get the cook up and send him to the mess hall. They could use one of the guest rooms in the BOQs for sleep.

Hammer had to think back to those football days to remember their appetites. He had forgotten just how much they used to eat until watching Bill. Hammer didn't even think the napkins were safe, especially with Bill being foodless for a week or more. Bill ate just about everything in sight and then, like an old bear with a full stomach, wanted some rest. He was half asleep when the MPs led the two of them to the BOQs. They were given a room with two beds and a bathroom. Hammer couldn't imagine Bill taking a shower with most of his head taped and gauze all around his left hand and ribs. He led his beaten friend to a bed and let him fall in place. He was out cold in a matter of seconds.

Hammer was tired too. At almost fifty-nine, the hike to the lodge and back to the plane was about all that he was up for. His knees hurt, his hips hurt, his hands were all cut up and his ankles were iced and bandaged. If that wasn't enough, Hammer was still ticked off about the holes in his airplane. Resigning to the fact that everything still worked on his own body, not having found any major cuts or gouges needing stitches, he hit the shower and then bed. He thought he would have to endure the noise Bill was broadcasting from his deep sleep, but he was fast asleep almost as fast as Bill had been.

The morning came too soon for the two and they awoke to the sounds of an active base. Bill and Hammer were awakened by MPs and escorted to the mess hall for chow. As they passed other civilian and military men carrying their equipment and preparing for action, they both received nods in respect. The instant bonding brought back memories of old military preparations, being included as a major part of combat in Vietnam, incentive for making their stiff and sore bodies more eager to get to the lodge.

When the combination of military, local law officers and the two tired warriors finished eating, they all went to the airfield where two Cessna 206s, two helicopters and Hammer's plane were waiting. The military officers and a squad of armed MPs. would take the helicopters. The local officers had chartered the two 206s from the local FBO for their men. Their own pilots would fly them to the lake. Hammer would be flying his plane, even with the patch job. The FBI was scheduled to fly out of Anchorage and meet them at the lodge. Hammer had a feeling that the FBI would soon be in charge of the whole operation, the other organizations were just not equipped for handling this size of a force. It was more in the realm of the FBI than the military, even though both had the fire power needed to go against the terrorists with automatic weapons.

At eight thirty, the flight from King Salmon was off under a less than 4,000-foot overcast, a better than typically good Alaskan day.

The motley looking bunch of aircraft were in a parade formation, with two U-H 1 Hueys leading the pack, two 206s in the middle and Hammer's plane flying the tail position like a mother hen. Hammer had to back off the power a bit, as did the 206s to keep in formation. Hopefully, with all of the various law enforcement organizations moving toward the lodge, there might be enough fire power.

Mark had received a call from his boss letting him know that the military had been alerted to some possible terrorist activity in the state. He jumped at the news and arranged for a phone line to the debriefing. Near the end of the call, arrangements were made for a time and place to meet the next morning. The FBI would leave from Anchorage and meet the military and civilian group from King Salmon at the lodge. Evidently the military police thought they could handle the terrorists. If there was any doubt, a flight of two F-15s would be circling above them. Mark immediately got on the phone and scheduled two choppers with range and speed enough to take his teams to the lodge. He then contacted the closest two teams to meet at the hangar on the south side of Anchorage International Airport at seven thirty sharp in the morning. He advised them to bring their gear.

At seven fifteen the FBI teams met and loaded aboard the choppers. They departed sharply at seven thirty, flying directly to Kenai, crossing Cook Inlet and then west along the northern coastline of the inlet. Mark had never seen the area up close by air and was astonished; the amount of water, high mountains and rough country was enormous. Catching any al-Qaeda cell would be practically impossible, he thought while looking out over the primitive area in this small portion of the state. During the first introductions to his new team, he was unaware of the ruggedness of the terrain his members would be up against. Seeing the countryside up close for the first time gave Mark a new outlook. His thinking that information would and should be easy to obtain would no longer hold true. No wonder the reports were slowly coming in.

Flying over the southeast shore line of Lake Iliamna, Mark was again impressed by the enormity of water and height of the mountains.

The lodge soon appeared and they landed next to two Hueys already on the ground. Radio contact with the MPs had informed them that the hostiles were gone. The FBI members retrieved their gear from the choppers and went to work finding forensic evidence and collecting information and any other clues that might reveal the identities of the men who had taken over the lodge. Mark, and his team member Dean from St. Louis, walked the entire lodge area and after giving instructions to his teams, he and Dean spent little time on the scene and soon left for Anchorage.

In Anchorage, Mark drove back to his office from the airport. He grabbed a handful of mail from his box, casually thumbing through the stack, not really concentrating on what was in front of him. His mind was on what he had seen at the lodge. The coffee was just warm, but better than nothing, so he added his typical two packages of Equal and powdered cream, swirling the brew with a finger. His desk was a mess and he took a few minutes to clear the papers covering everything. Reaching for the land line, Mark dialed a familiar number. The phone came alive with the four pulse tones of a secure line and soon a voice answered: "Agent Berry, FBI."

Mark had called an old partner in the St. Louis unit. "Stan, this is Mark. They're here."

The trip from King Salmon to the lodge was made in average time with a good tailwind and the overcast about 4,000 feet. The Hueys landed on the flat area near the lodge and Hammer and Bill made an approach, landing on the nearby strip behind the 206s. They left the plane in the turn around and began the quarter-mile walk to the lodge. They were almost to the front door when they heard the whine of two Dauphin Aerospatiale helicopters. The FBI teams landed close to the two Hueys and unloaded their equipment. Hammer and Bill set out to look for any signs of the cook and Bill's dogs, which were nowhere in sight. Bill kept calling with no results.

The lodge did not appear to be badly disrupted, but the signs of a large group of people were quite obvious. There were trays of dirty glasses, plates and food around. Most importantly, the building and equipment were still usable. The whole lodge was swept for explosives and inspected for traps. The group of men obviously left in a hurry. The generator was started and Hammer and Bill checked a few of the smaller out buildings, finding nothing of significance. Bill told the military police where the stash of mines was. As they were checking out the last out building, a radio call came in from another unit on the lake side of the lodge. An area of a suspicious nature had been found and their presence had been requested.

Bill and Hammer headed for the lake passing across two small cleared fields, covered with several bear carcasses and many other smaller animals, all in pieces; probably used for explosive training.

The area they were called to was a shallow gravesite. Several of the military personnel were digging around as the FBI agents supervised. The shallowness of the trench indicated that the people who originally dug it were in a hurry and didn't care if it was found. When the agents finished digging, the shallow trench revealed the bodies of two dogs, two men and the remnants of skin and bone from other animals, somewhat deeper and probably what was left from the skinned animals in the shed.

One of the bodies was the cook, with a bullet hole in the forehead. The other body was a scruffy-looking man, also with a bullet hole in the forehead. By the looks of a large bruise on one side of the face, he appeared to be the guard that Hammer had belted with his rifle butt. The body of the cook had been seriously burned. Bill showed his emotions by pacing at the edge of the grave. His dogs and friend had been killed and he had done nothing about it. This small grave seemed to be a message and was just a portion of the real damage to the area.

The rest of the beautiful precious wilderness overlooking and surrounding Bill's lodge he treasured so much and had kept pristine was viciously killed and gutted to the last bird and squirrel for no reason. If they had not eaten it, animals and birds had been killed for the fun of it, carcasses lying beneath the trees and bushes. His lodge and business had been violated. There was nothing Bill could do at this time but pace and think of retribution, even in his state of dilapidation.

The FBI had pointed out various areas of cleared land. Some was from the detonation of high explosive devices and others were for ranges and obstacle courses. Wherever one looked, there was an animal carcass in pieces.

Whoever these guys were, they left in a hurry and were kind enough to not leave more mines. In the days that the cell had taken over, they had managed a large amount of excavation. Hammer assumed that they might have had the help of the grader, but a good percentage was done by hand. There was still no clue to the identity of the intruders. Bill continued to help disarm the mines and he put them in well marked cardboard boxes. Hammer kept well clear of the devices. Even in 'nam, he stayed on base most of the time to keep away from mines and booby traps. He had seen too many of his friend's lose limbs and lives from of the ugly shrapnel-filled killers.

Bill and Hammer met back at the small building where Bill had been rescued. They checked the contents and then headed to Bill's office at the lodge. Hammer couldn't figure out Bill's motives until seeing him press a hidden switch that opened a secret safe room; the two could only smile. Bill told him that the first day his guests arrived they had asked him to put some valuables in the safe. Since then, the bad guys had tried to gain entry, but the door to the safe was unknown to the guests. Hammer knew now why they had kept Bill alive--to get back in the safe. The little room with the large safe would be Hammer and Bill's little secret for now. They would find out more about the situation and what kind of help they would receive from the authorities before disclosing all of their information. Bill closed the hidden door and he and Hammer headed outside to where the FBI agents were gathered.

The two couldn't do anything more at the lodge so they told the FBI agents to lock the doors when they left and that the two of them would be back with a crew for cleaning and disposing of the animal carcasses in a few days. "Take what you need or what was important" was the last comment from Bill. The two headed for the generator building to add fuel to the large tank.

Hammer and Bill filled the generator tank with fuel and then walked to the plane. Hammer added forty gallons of 100 octane low-lead in 78 Bravo and they climbed aboard, got airborne and headed direct to Dillingham. Bill would stay with Hammer for the time being and then fly to Anchorage to recruit help to piece back his lodge. Hammer just wanted to get home to the girls. The adventure had taken a toll on his body and mind and he wanted to get rid of the stiffness with a dip in the hot tub.

Bill was what one would call a loud sleeper. A train would be hard pressed to be louder. During the flight home, Hammer almost had to wake him up to just talk on the radio.

After putting the plane in the hangar and driving to the house, Hammer gave Bill the penthouse suite, the room above the garage that he used for his home theater. It had a hide-a-bed that was comfortable and a refrigerator stocked with drinks and jerky. This was pig's heaven for Bill. He could hold up in that room for a long time.

On the other hand, Hammer still had a business to run. He really didn't know how the customers would feel about the holes or patches in the plane, but was sure he could conjure up some story like, "The holes happened while I was cleaning my gun." He called British Columbia about the second plane and was told, it would be ready in two to four weeks, depending on whether he wanted the rush job or not. Hammer opted for four weeks and told them to take their time. He wanted their best job. He also had to call the insurance agent in Anchorage. Hammer hoped bullet holes were covered by his policy.

The holes were covered, so he arranged with Anchorage Aircraft Supply, a Cessna parts supplier, to ship some new panels and look for some other used parts without holes. The 336 was an older plane and used parts would not be hard to find. Hammer received a call from his friend at the FAA who had heard from the FBI. He was interested in the adventure. Hammer called back and told him he would tell his story over lunch the next day when he was in Anchorage.

CHAPTER 8

By the time Hammer had finished with all of the insurance matters and ordering parts for repairing the plane, he was anxious to head home. He had spent little time with the girls and they wanted to know all about the lodge adventure. He made up a great story and sent them to watch a movie. He told Sandy the real story and her only reply was, "I wish I would have been there." Hammer had already guessed what she would say; it was just like her "macho grunt attitude." He hit the sack early; the next day would be filled with a trip for two passengers to Anchorage and a return with freight.

One of the busiest times of the year, Hammer depended on the frantic demands of his customers for a good profit and to also try and add new clients. Hammer had to satisfy his clients or, in the current market, lose whatever he had. If his efforts failed, one of the other companies would graciously be there to take his business. He wasn't about to let that happen, as he wasn't about to let those terrorists take potshots at him. He had a family to think of and protect. His thinking moved from his accounts, mostly on the business, to a concern about repercussions from the cell. Sandy was confident in her abilities to protect the girls and Hammer knew she was capable. She would have to be the guardian at home and he would keep flying; hopefully the authorities would catch up with whoever was responsible for the destruction at the lodge.

The next day Hammer flew to Anchorage with his two passengers and met with his company insurance broker to discuss the damage to the airplane in more detail. A few pictures were snapped and the matter was quickly resolved. He was then off to meet with Jeff, his FAA friend, at the Tea Leaf restaurant. The two had served in the air force together and had become good friends. It was partly Jeff's idea for Hammer to buy the company in Dillingham. The two talked about the airplane and the lodge; this over a large bowl of hot sour soup, spiced a bit more with peppered oil and vinegar.

When someone shot at a plane, Jeff's job was to investigate and report the incident to the FBI. Charges were stiff when breaking that law. At first glance, Jeff patted Hammer on the back, stating, "By the holes and their placement, the ones covered by patches, you are lucky to be alive."

Hammer assured him not to worry about his business and certificate, the holes would be patched and the structure of the plane was sound. They shook hands and said their farewells, Jeff heading to his office at the airport to call the FBI and Hammer to pick up his load of cargo. Hammer didn't know how the customers would take to the patches on the airplane, but so far, they had not been scared off; to the contrary, they just wanted some information or a good story. The story had also been passed along to the pilots in the area. The chain of gossip, word of mouth connecting the local pilots, was much better than a front page article in the newspaper.

Hammer remained tightlipped and wasn't going to talk anymore to anyone about the events at the lodge, at least not until he had found out more of the facts. Eventually, he just avoided the topic altogether; the story was getting tedious and repetitive. Tired of his activities being disrupted and a bit grumpy, the last straw was having the FBI call. They had called for a meeting, which Hammer questioned as more of a social attempt at getting information. They couldn't care less about Bill or his health.

Hammer drove to a weathered brick building in downtown Anchorage, parked, and then pushed his way through two heavy glass doors. A receptionist proved the barrier between further advances. He was asked for and provided identification, given a visitors badge and told to wait for an agent. By this time he was not only peeved, but well behind schedule; his inclination was to just leave, but in the nick of time an agent showed and walked Hammer back to a series of offices.

Introducing himself to Hammer, Mark stated a few facts and continued with questions about the lodge. Hammer was in no mood for the agent's attitude and presentation. His tone and lack of respect struck Hammer as a person he wanted no part of. He finally had enough of the agent's biting sarcasm and being fed trivial information. Standing quickly and then heading for the door, the agent realized his error. Having teases thrown for a means of holding the pilot's interest; the agent still probed. With a last ditch effort, the agent mentioned an "al-Qaeda cell" and some possible motives for them taking over the lodge. As for Hammer, his momentum toward the door was not interrupted and he made no effort to acknowledge what the FBI wanted or needed as he walked out.

Starting the truck and thinking of his next move, Hammer thought of his opinions. The FBI was interested in one thing for sure- -themselves--and would be no help to him. The agent mentioned an al-Qaeda cell, but the facts were not firm in Hammer's mind. Besides, what did a terrorist factor want with the lodge? He admitted to himself that he knew nothing of this group, only what he had read or heard from the news. The Feds had their job to do and they would have to find information and succeed without his help.

The load of produce was picked up at the warehouse: fresh fruit, vegetables, milk, thirty dozen donuts, and fifty frozen pizzas would go to Igigic. He also picked up some new clothes for Bill. With the finish of chores and on the way to the airport, Hammer estimated he would be back in Dillingham after dark. Ever since he had been in Alaska, it hadn't taken him long to analyze the flying; when you're done, your done! Whatever it takes, it takes!

Hammer called home and spoke to Sandy, letting her know his schedule and asking how the girls were. They weren't back from school, but she would let them know he called. Bill was probably charging up a huge bill on the satellite system and hadn't been out of the apartment all day. Hammer told Sandy that he would call again leaving Igigic. Plans for the next day included a full day in the hangar and a local mechanic helping with repairing what they could on the plane.

As Hammer prepared to leave Anchorage, he checked around the plane on the preflight inspection and replaced or added more tape where it was needed. The rudder was okay with a few adjustments. He added a quart of oil to the rear engine and checked the cargo compartment to make sure the doors were closed. Hooking up the power tug to the front wheel, he pulled 78 Bravo away from the hangars and positioned it for starting. He removed the tug and placed it back in the hangar, closing the doors with the outside key pad. Hammer climbed into the plane and went through his checklist. He started both engines and received his clearance to taxi. One more clearance for take-off and he was off to Igigic.

The store van was waiting at the airport and Hammer and the driver loaded the cargo in the van. He tried calling the house with no luck and figured they were out getting pizza. The flight to Dillingham was quick and at fifteen miles out from the airport he called the flight service and got the winds. At eight miles out he called for traffic advisory with his intentions and made a straight in landing. There was no other traffic. He taxied to his hangar, shutting down the master and mags, coasting to a spot near the large doors. With the remote, he opened the doors of the hangar and retrieved the tug, connecting it to the front wheel. Starting the little five-horsepower motor, he guided the tug back and forth, moving the plane to its position inside the hangar on the marked reference points painted on the floor. He loaded the truck with all of the remaining items from Anchorage and remotely shut the door. Returning to a key pad on the outside wall of the hangar, he shut the lights off, except the night light, locked the door and set the alarm. Hammer's six-foot three, 230-pound body was tired and ready for some sleep.

When he reached the turnoff for his driveway in front of the house, Hammer noticed the whole area was dark. There were no lights on at the house or the garage, not even the automatic lights that came on when the natural light had faded. His family must not be back from dinner. Hammer pulled in to the drive and up near the garage door. He turned the ignition off and withdrew the key, stepping out of the cab. Where was Francis? She always came to meet him. She must be with the dinner group. By now he started to feel that something was wrong. The hair on the back of his neck was standing straight out. He had no weapon and no light. Hammer could make out a couple of dark forms out of place on the porch. They had no particular definition in the dark. His night vision would take another few minutes to kick in.

As he slowly moved to the house, using a sweeping motion he grabbed the potato fork from the garden and continued to the porch, every one of his senses at peak awareness. There was something large and different on the porch all right, and the front door looked partially open. He moved steadily and slowly, poised with the fork, moving around the obstructions and edging sideways through the front door. Moving into the house, he found another large object just inside the door in the hall. He reached for the lights and flipped them on. Nothing happened. He couldn't see a thing so he backtracked to the outside, heading for the side of the garage and the breaker box. The main handle had been placed in the "off" position so he flipped it "on," and the surrounding lights illuminated the house.

CHAPTER 9

The lights came on and Hammer spent little time moving back to the house. The front porch light accented one of the forms he had almost tripped over on the porch. It was the body of a strange man, surrounded by a rather large pool of blood. The gore in the hallway was also another man. Hammer didn't recognize either one. Both were shot two times in the chest. He started to panic and yelled for the girls.

Immediately he heard a commotion from upstairs, with the scramble of feet and the yelling of high-pitched fear. "Daddy! Daddy!" The girls sprinted down the stairs to Hammer's arms. He was inundated with sobs and cheers. He moved them away from the bodies and into the living room to ask questions. The first thing they said was that Sandy had been hurt and needed help so the three of them ran up the stairs and to the back closet in the bedroom. Hammer found Sandy with a little blood on her head and a gimpy leg.

"What happened to you? Who are these guys? What did they want?" Hammer was in a state of shock. They were all in a state of shock!

"Three guys tried to get in and only two made it," Sandy replied. The first man evidently got a taste of her black belt with an unexpected groin kick and a round house that connected ankle and head, sending him into the glass of the front door and shattering it into a million pieces. "He staggered back out the door while two others tried to come in." In a quivering voice she said, "I shot them."

Hammer unemotionally announced with an emphatic tone, "Yes you did, and very well."

Hammer left the bedroom and went down the stairs, telling the girls to stay with Sandy. She still had her pistol. He checked the rest of the house and stepped over the body in the hallway, exiting to the porch. Again he called, "Francis!" with no luck and then headed for the garage. Hammer moved slowly up the stairs to the dark little room above the garage with potato fork in hand, sliding the spare key from his truck ring in the door lock and opening it slowly. He didn't notice any damage except one of the little windows in the door was broken. He flipped the lights on, expecting to see Bill's bloody body on the floor.

The apartment was empty. Hammer called out. There was a slight rustling coming from the back side of the couch and Hammer heard the sounds of a stiff body moaning and standing. Bill appeared from the shadows.

"Are you all right" Hammer asked.

With a nod of the head, Bill gave him a sheepish smile. "Yeah, I'm okay," he said.

Hammer turned and headed back down the stairs to the truck, again with potato fork in hand. Opening the door, he grabbed the handheld VHF radio and made a call to the flight service on the air field, asking them to send help and the paramedics. He had noticed that the phone lines had been cut at the utility box. His sat phone was in the hangar. He had thought of getting a cell phone, but towers were few and far between, making the sat phone the best source of communication.

With the power back, Hammer pressed the small rectangular remote in the truck, triggering the motor that lifted the hefty door panels. He quickly headed for the opening door, triggering automatic lights that activated as he entered their field of detection. At the back wall he moved a small panel, exposing a key pad. Punching in four numbers, he heard a loud click and then a large steel door partially opened. Some effort was needed to open the door far enough to gain entrance to a small room that contained a huge gun safe, the walk-in type. He spun the tumblers and opened the safe door, removing two hand guns, a pump-style shotgun and a bandolier of magnum triple-O buckshot shells. He closed the door snuggly.

Bill was almost down the stairs by now and as Hammer moved past him to the house, he handed him the shotgun and shells. "Who were those guys anyway?" Hammer asked.

Bill strained to catch up in stride, eventually marching to the house while describing what had happened. He had recognized two of the five men getting out of a dark SUV at the side of the house. They were part of the group of terrorists from the lodge. The driveway sensor had tripped when they approached and Bill had thought it might be Hammer. Surprised to see the two men he could recognize, he called Sandy on the intercom to alert her. Hammer was thankful because the call had probably saved the girls' and Sandy's lives.

The two men walked back into the main house, stepping around the bodies. Bill inquired about Sandy and the girls. Hammer gave him the diver's okay sign, a thumbs-up, and they climbed the stairs to wait for the police together.

From the second story they could hear the sirens blaring and see lights flashing. With little emotion remaining, having used up all of their adrenaline, the thought of help being on the way was satisfying. However, to Sandy and the girls, Hammer and Bill, together, provided a calming demeanor. There was no need for anyone else.

While they answered the questions of the local law-enforcement officers, Sandy told them that when she received the call from Bill she moved to the front hall and locked the door just as a foot kicked it in. That's when she had gone into action.

Over in the apartment, two other men broke a window to gain entry. Startled by the shots, they sprinted down the stairs and fled in the SUV. Bill had been waiting by the door in the dark with Hammer's Edgar Martinez-autographed bat and was about to hit a double when he was also startled by the shots. The noise triggered an instinct to take cover and he did behind the couch where Hammer had found him.

Hammer questioned the motives of the men that were lying on the porch. "How did they know where to find the house? Maybe from the airplane number?" He knew the task was easy with a computer and the correct Internet address. Hammer was tired, but flying higher than a kite on adrenaline.

He had enough of these guys. No more being casual or ignorant about the motives they had shown toward his family. Maybe the words of the FBI agent meant something. Were they al-Qaeda? At least now they had faces to identify them. They were murderers and he knew his family had been lucky this time. Ignorance was no excuse for learning the hard way. They had killed at the lodge and had the same intentions for him. They must have thought no one would get in their way. They were wrong this time, not expecting any action from Sandy.

Where would Hammer take his family now? They couldn't stay here. They would have to move somewhere safe if there was such a place. In the morning Hammer would call the FBI and tell them about the intruders. He and Sandy could do more on their own. The authorities could not help, being in Anchorage and so far away. Now, he had to take care of the girls himself.

The police and paramedics finished their work, removing the bodies and taking pictures and collecting evidence. Sandy and the girls were given a ride to a downtown motel by the police. Besides a couple of pools of blood and the two doors needing fixing, the house was none the worse for wear. Hammer went back to the gun safe and got a couple more guns and a rifle along with ammunition. He locked the garage and started a last-minute check around the front of the house. Bill took the back.

Hammer stopped for a moment to jot down a note to himself:

Contact the phone company.
Contact the FBI.
Talk to insurance Co.

Suddenly he heard a shout from Bill who was near the back of the house, between the garden and the garage. As Hammer came closer, he recognized a mound of fur. It was Francis. She didn't have a chance with a bullet hole in the head. How would Hammer tell the girls? He needed to find these guys and now. He was in a momentary rage and needing to calm down. Hammer vowed to himself that there would be no stopping him once he found the low lives responsible. He would eliminate whoever they were, no matter how long it took.

The answers and solutions to Hammer's emotional outbursts were not going to be remedied by the FBI or any other law-enforcement organization. His experience told him he was on his own on this one. If he talked to the FBI, they would just say "Come on in and we'll talk about it" or "We're working on it." No doubt the FBI and other authorities were, but not fast enough for him. He could not and would not leave his family in danger, waiting for the authorities to act. Especially with an organization totally void of American law. He had connections in the area and would use every one of them to keep his family safe. Hammer decided he would do everything in his power to find this so-called cell. He would need Bill's help.

The helicopter could be found and tracked to someone or some company. It needed fuel and others would have seen it. Bill had to get better to help him. Rambo, he was not. If Hammer started something, he wanted to be able to finish it, just like his rescue at the lodge. He would hide his family in a safe place. He would leave the truck in the garage and get a rental. He would also move the plane tomorrow. It was vulnerable.

Hammer's mind was a blur of emotions, running on adrenaline and needing sleep. He had to overcome his want for retribution and his feeling of being violated and start thinking clearly with detailed planning using his "common sense" mind and not his emotion. Terrorists were just that and he knew what they had done. They had implanted the image that they could easily get to his loved ones and even him. He was susceptible to the negative and started to feel helpless. This was not his way. He had to go after them. He would find them, no matter what.

Mark wasn't surprised when a call came in from the local Dillingham police that night. Two bodies were found after an attack on the house owner. The name was Carpenter. Was it coincidence or were there other Carpenters in the area? He expected retribution from the cell, but not within a few days. He should have warned the two men, but most cells just wanted to move on with little attention. He would send the King Salmon team over to Dillingham to investigate and do the forensics. They could also collect the bodies and bring them back to Anchorage. Mark made a note to gather more information about the lodge owner and the pilot.

The cell finding Hammer's house, the violent intrusion, killing Francis plus the dead at Bill's lodge was too much to accept. Hammer worried, not so much about his company, the maintenance, insurance, customers and time; they all seemed trivial at this point. His pride and joy had become afterthought. Now it was the safety of his family he was mostly concerned with. If the cell found them once, the cell could find them again. The FBI would just hide them in a safe house and not get rid of the real problem. There was only one solution and that was to eliminate the threat.

PART 2

PREPARATION FOR RETRIBUTION

Striking Back

CHAPTER 10

Bill hitched a ride with Hammer on his next flight to Anchorage. This provided the necessary time for the two to come up with a course of action and discuss just how far they were willing to commit themselves. They agreed that they could not assume the task of finding and dealing with terrorists on their own. Even though the appropriate authorities were supposedly handling the situation, they both knew that the two of them would stand a better chance dealing with the cell directly and not waiting for the authorities. They knew the local area and were free to roam about, not hampered by procedures and regulations that would slow the process. They had their own agenda.

It seemed that the FBI was having difficulty sifting through what little information and evidence they had found. Their computers were coming up blank. They received very little, if any, cooperation from other agencies and the result was remaining clueless to the culprits. The police had no idea what was going on either; none of the agencies were communicating with each other. They only had the outcome of the pilot's house and the lodge for evidence and no other agency shared. It appeared that there was an authority issue, every agency wanted the lead!

During the flight and after all of their conversation and brainstorming, the two decided that when they talked to the agencies they would be tightlipped with what information they did have. This way, they would keep from being another target and be one step ahead. They wanted the ability to strike first.

Very little time was needed to come up with the idea to establish a team and both Hammer and Bill had numerous friends who might be helpful gathering a list of possible members; experts in the field who hired themselves out for this type of project. They needed the best men available for reconnaissance and aggressive combat. The members would have to be a step above the ordinary mercenary. Vowing secrecy and confidentiality was a large part of the job requirements. After all, they both would be hanging out on that proverbial limb if they were caught. Each member would know the ramifications to an operation of this type. Penalties would be stiff from the authorities.

At first, candidates would be found through their military friends. Bill would be in Anchorage calling his stateside friends and Hammer would do the same, either from Dillingham or wherever he might be. Hammer and Bill both agreed that they could sponsor a small team for a short time with the money they had at hand. Neither of the two were naïve. They both knew that their style of life, the carefree family life of Hammer's and the backcountry easy life of Bill's, was over for the time being and maybe forever.

Bill was adamant about getting back to the lodge. He told Hammer that the safe was important and they needed to take possession of the contents as soon as possible. Both Hammer and Bill were not going to be left out of the informational loop. Together they had agreed that the local authorities might need whatever help they could get. The two were anxious, wanting to see just what the group of men was planning. Bill wasn't exactly sure what was left in the safe or even if the safe was still intact since they had left, but he did know there was something important of value there. The trip to the lodge would be in the morning.

What was important for Hammer was to get back to his family. The safe would have to wait. He was sure the girls were out of danger, but would take no chances .Sandy was good at protecting them, but she still had a bum ankle. Sandy had plenty of fire power with her pistols and the Remington 11-87 Magnum Police auto loader.

That evening, Hammer had a chance for some deep thinking and who he might call. In Anchorage, Bill was more successful and able to find several of his old ex-military friends who could help, just the type they were looking for. He was also successful getting medical help for the abuse he took from the beatings. What bones could be tended to and a few loose and broken teeth were looked at. As he was poked and prodded, he continued obtaining names of other experienced young men that would be valuable for any type of aggressive operations. He and hammer were no longer young pups, spry and able to recuperate quickly. They needed trained fresh eyes and ears. They also needed people who had the ability to maintain an advantage over any combat situation. They could keep up, but to have young well-toned muscles and trained senses would improve the odds for success.

Hammer found only two who were able and willing to come to Anchorage at the moment. The first, a friend of an ex-flying buddy from Tucson, was a flier and was more than willing to help his old CO. The second, a real find, was an ex-spook from Langley. He was a friend of a friend who had done work for his ex-commanding officer from Cannon. The CO said he would check him out from that end and get back to Hammer. Meanwhile, Hammer would make inquiries of his own about the two.

Hammer pulled into the driveway of his house and scanned for observers. Seeing none, he headed directly to the garage and his safe. He picked out a few pieces from his prize gun collection and adequate ammo for the weapons. Most were unfired and some were collector's items by serial number, a rarity. He also had a few specialty weapons that had been ported and silenced. He opted for several Glock 9 mm's and his old warhorse, the two .40 caliber Sigs. Hopefully they wouldn't be needed, but he wanted to make sure he was prepared.

Hammer bought most of his guns from a friend who owned a sports store in the area. He might have the stock he was looking for, the most modern and advanced automatic weapons. Although they were illegal, the weapons were needed to be equalizers to what the terrorists had. Before closing the safe, Hammer pulled out a newly

Dana L. Coy

acquired, easily concealable Walther PPK for insurance. He placed all of the weapons in his daypack, along with two boxes of Remington hollow points for each and two extra magazines. He secured the safe and walked the entire yard again. Setting the alarms was the last thing before heading to the backyard and burying Francis. He was not looking forward to the task, but with a sad heart and a fire in his eyes, he finished the job and then headed for town.

Briefly conversing with Sandy and the girls, Hammer left for the airport about seven in the evening. The motel Sandy and the girls stayed in was located a few hundred feet from the police station. This gave Hammer a little piece of mind and helped with his thinking as he continued to write down ideas and plans. He scribbled in a small notebook as he flew over the mountains and Cook Inlet. Names, times, events, appearances, everything he could remember about Bill's lodge would be important. He was certain that information would eventually be the key to the downfall of the cell. Hammer chastised himself for being so unprepared. His education, combat experience, and knowing the characteristics of people like these terrorists from his 'nam experiences all meant squat if he could not protect his family. There was so much to get even for and he didn't even know who to get even with.

Hammer met Bill at the hotel in Anchorage and they ordered room service before starting on a long night's work. Expecting to spend several hours laying out any possible strategies for a team, the two men started by systematically comparing pages of notes they both had written, trying to identify members of the cell. From the discussion and any facts they had come up with, they concluded that the men could actually be indeed a rogue al-Qaeda cell. From the language, weapons and methods they used, it was not difficult to come to that conclusion. There was actually no other explanation.

The terrorist cell was not going to stop what they were doing or planning and with the information Bill was hoping for, the material in the safe, there was a good chance to get the upper hand on them and rid the area of this faction.

The two concluded their discussion by talking about personnel for the team and what each had found, finishing the evening with cleaning and preparing the weapons for the next day.

The early wake-up call came at 5:00 A.M. and was much different from the days before at King Salmon. They were both up at the sound of the ring and ready to go in very little time. Stopping for a coffee on the way to the airport, the Skymaster had been fueled and they were in the air before six, managing to get to the lodge in less than two hours. The typical headwinds were fifteen knots. The place looked alive from the air. The generator was still running, supplying the electricity for the lights, a ruse to fool anyone that the lodge was occupied. They would find out if the deception had worked when they landed.

Hammer guided the plane to the center line in a slight crosswind, touching down and taxiing to the turn around. He cut the remaining engine. The cloud cover was about 2,500 feet and had dropped slightly since Augustine Island. The headwind and drizzle would last the entire day. The two armed themselves and stealthily made their way from the airstrip to the back side of the lodge, surmising that anyone there would have heard the plane. Bill was slow with a sling and bandaged ribs. He was also without pain being helped by a number of pain killers. Hammer had tried to make the landing as quietly as possible, shutting down one engine five miles out.

Bill carried his favorite revolver, a Smith & Wesson model 29 with a six-inch barrel. The .44 magnum was more his style—big and loud. For the heavy work, he also carried a twelve-gauge three-inch magnum shotgun loaded with seven rounds of triple-ought buckshot. Hammer had his .45-70, not a small round either, and his trusty Sig .40 cal. They were still no match for automatic weapons. The yellow tape was in place near the shallow gravesite and other areas of importance surrounding the lodge. Fortunately, they found no evidence of anyone being there since the FBI had left. Hammer kept a keen sense and a sharp eye for mines.

The mines had been swept and it appeared that the lodge had not been disturbed since they had left. The hidden door and safe had managed to slip by the authorities. Bill opened the back door to the lodge and the interior offered an eerie silence. Only the slight hum of a refrigerator and the outside generator could be heard. The two went from room to room, examining the entire lodge, meeting in the back office. Bill grabbed a few cold Red Bulls from the refrigerator on the way and tossed a couple to Hammer when they met.

Bill pressed the magic keys of a hidden pad and a panel popped open, very much like Hammer's' garage safe. A 6 foot x 4 foot x 6 foot vault, bolted to the floor in the small area, was the center of attraction. Bill retrieved a key from above the door jamb and unlocked the tumblers. He whirled the dial, aligning the numbered discs, and then turned the large wheel that retracted a series of round bars, allowing the safe door to be opened.

Hammer wasn't expecting much, probably just an empty safe, but to the contrary, there were packets of Bill's' money and papers. There was also a large attaché case with a packet of portfolios bound to one side and an army duffle bag, secured by a lock. It looked like a major gold strike. They carefully opened the attaché case and were surprised to find it full of papers and documents. At first glance, understanding what appeared to be Arabic would be the most difficult and did not disclose what they had discovered. They would check the locked duffle later. Their interest lay in the portfolios and hopefully, when interpreted, the contents might lead them to the people they were looking for.

Casually thumbing through the files, the case was found to be full of pictures and information indicating striking points including the pipe line, the Air force base and several canneries. Some files were in English, but most were in a strange language. The team would need someone who could read and speak the unfamiliar script. Neither of them spoke a word of anything other than English. Bill spoke a little Vietnamese, not much use now.

After all the effort, both were getting impatient and like a Labrador retriever after duck, Hammer, quivering and shaking, wanted to know simply who the bad guys were and where he could find them. Bill knew Hammer was getting frustrated and almost out of control. However, to continue this project, logically working to find the cell, he needed Hammer in full mental control. They were both anxious to cross swords with the terrorists, but Bill offered a few brotherly suggestions to settle Hammer down and the mood became more productive and less emotional.

The two men carried the attaché, files, and the duffle bag to the plane and then inspected the lodge again before locking it. Bill had his money and papers. Then the men put more fuel in the generator tank and locked the shed. The generator would now run for another two weeks. They would be back again by then. At the strip, Hammer topped off the plane's tanks and loaded a few bags of clothes for Bill, along with the contents of the safe.

They departed, still not knowing how much information they had or who they were looking for. They were anxious to get on the trail.

The mood was not jovial , but dark in tone while the twosome, singing the made-up lyrics to the old pirate song *Dead Man's Chest,* referring to the attaché case they had just retrieved, flew back to Anchorage and a first meeting with the new team of men. Snapping the lids and downing a couple of more Red Bulls, they filled the sky with made-up verses to old songs, depicting their mood and the situation at hand for about a half hour. The rest of the trip was spent deciding who they should share their newly acquired information with and then finally Bill's snoring. Hammer didn't mind. The sound would not bother him through his headset and he would communicate any new thoughts to Bill later.

Arriving at their hotel in Anchorage, a note had been left at the desk for Hammer and he dialed the hand-scribbled number on the courtesy phone. He waited for just two rings before an answer and he then invited the voice on the other end of the phone to meet in his room.

He and Bill enlisted a bellman and his cart to help with the bags from the lodge. The timing was perfect and as soon as he and Bill finished a quick cleanup they heard a quiet knock. Hammer opened the door and two middle-aged men walked in and introduced themselves. The four exchanged names and identification and talked briefly, trying to break whatever uneasiness was between them.

The gesture of exchanging identification was meaningless. Hammer explained the situation. All four seemed to come to a common understanding of what was happening and the requirements for the employment. Being military and veterans, they each shared distaste for organizations like al-Qaeda. The new recruits possessed the perfect knowledge and experience, making them a perfect match with what Hammer and Bill needed and they finished the formalities with an agreement for compensation.

Excitement in the room grew as the four men told of their backgrounds. They shared a meal and finally finished the evening with work, examining the booty from Bill's safe. Much more information was discovered than they ever would have thought. This had been a major foul-up by the now known cell. Hammer and Bill listened as one of the new members translated the Arabic. The few read reports were significant in that they revealed just exactly what the cell's intentions were.

With the surprising amount of revealing information in hand and

left at the lodge, the four discussed their next step.

Meeting as a team and talking about taking the law in their own hands was, in essence, being another rogue cell in itself. This though was brought up by "Spook," one of the new members, as he presented the dilemma. Hammer thought, "Yes, we are a rogue cell and highly illegal, but if that's what it takes to confront these terrorists, I see no other option." The word *terrorist* infuriated Hammer to no end and he was feeling the impact. He hated to be threatened and bullied. The consensus of all of the team members was to hound the cell till extinction.

"Should we turn the material over to the FBI or handle it our own way?" Hammer had presented the question for discussion. This was the most important topic before any other plans could be made, a first test of their material to establish confidence; they all agreed to wait until it was fully translated.

Spending their time compiling and organizing information was their first step. With enough clear factual data, a plan of action could be formed. Making up their minds not to involve the FBI, to notify them only when there was a need, would be made at a later date; emphasis was placed on a *need*.

This day was the first of many for Hammer, showing progress toward finding al-Qaeda cell and the leaders. Hammer and Bill, still pressured by what they thought of as a lifestyle of being hunted since the recue at the lodge, had nothing but optimism in mind and a future that showed a promise of again living their normal life. Of course, by being above the law, a one-way road was established. That one-way road, soon to begin, presented an indicator for either their demise or the opposite, a means for returning to a normal life. Whatever methods they chose for their destiny, whether good or bad, eliminating that flip of the coin for a more controllable outcome, the new team members all seemed to be thinking in the same direction, supplying ideas for acceptable methods and high percentages for success. Hammer and Bill were not only growing in confidence with the additional support and insights from new members, but also growing in enthusiasm, knowing at least who they were hunting. They would put an end to being threatened by terrorists and would see to their revenge.

CHAPTER 11

Mark was still exasperated with the progress of his teams. The few items of evidence—fingerprints, blood, and paperwork retrieved from the lodge—had not been helpful in finding the identification of the terrorists. He was unable to get any names from the FBI's national and international data base. There should have been much more forensics, but the lodge was a sloppy mess and contaminated by the number of people that walked through the structure in the last few days. They should have been able to find at least one person of interest. The teams working outside the city were also coming up empty-handed. In Dutch Harbor, any information collected was virtually useless; the companies all checked out as legitimate. It was the same for Kodiak, Cold Bay, King Cove, and Sand Point. The owners were good citizens, taxpayers, and their books were in order. Mark was frustrated and showed anger as he addressed his unit with threats during the weekly meeting. He needed information now!

The next day Hammer and his team were hard at work with the contents of the attaché. Stacks of paper lay on the bed in the motel room with the four pawing through, trying to decipher any meaning. After being translated to English and writing notes, individual piles were established for titles. Being the businessman as he was, Hammer worried about paying the hired help. He had volunteered his savings to get through this difficult time as had Bill. During the frenzy of looking through the paperwork, one of the members brought up the obvious subject of the duffle bag.

The three patiently watched as Bill pried the lock open, separating the canvas tabs. He turned the open end upside down on a clear portion of a bed and emptied the contents. To the amazement of the onlookers, a massive amount of money was revealed. They all paused and, as if at the starting gate of a race and on the first sound, they each grabbed a stack of cash and began counting.

The total was near a staggering $2 million. Hammer said, "This should put a damper on the terrorist's activity." Most of the bills were large. They checked for counterfeit, but the bills were all legitimate. The team had theorized that the money was for the individual operators, an amount given out enabling the purchase of anything anyplace. The terrorists were serious and well-funded.

Bill and Hammer eyed each other and immediately knew that the problem of funding the team was solved. Bill's statement was, "We know who is going to sponsor our team: the bad guys." The large bills would be a problem, but with the expertise of the team, particularly Bill's, they would make it work.

Bill spent several days working on how he could launder more and more money. Finally, enough money from the bag was processed to help with the expensive items, but Hammer and Bill's savings were used to offset the money needed for all of the equipment, giving them the time to complete the whole exchange.

The team now had a purpose, a sponsor, and a direction. There would be more new members joining the team in the next few days. Investigating the locations and the names mentioned in the files was the priority, with the surveillance starting as soon as the teams could purchase the equipment they needed. Hammer started his own research using the theory that the cell would be setting up other camps in the region like at Bill's lodge. He would talk to other pilots and ask them to look for strange or unusual activities on their routes. Any information would help. A number was set up for reporting any unusual sightings from other pilots. Informational cards were made to distribute to Hammer's pilot friends. All of the information received from the calls or conversation was kept in a log.

The general public was of no help, they just did not have the eyes in the sky the pilots had.

Within the next two days, the whole team was in place and a full-scale intelligence operation was in progress. Follow-ups, phone calls, computer work, all from known information, revealed several suspect companies. The ultimate goal was to find out whom and where the cell members were and if they were still using the peninsula for cover. Hammer was getting information from his pilot friends in two days. His notebook of sightings, locations, and dates was getting filled.

En route from King Salmon to Chignick — saw smoke coming from the old Thompson homestead. No one has lived there for four years. Alt. 1500.

Kirk May-15

Coming back from Perryville, observed people and smoke at the old Thompson place. Alt. 2000.

Ken May-15

King Salmon to Kodiak, low level through Katmai area. Saw -some activity had taken place near vacant lodge ten miles south of Hygrade strip. Noticed used paths and fog or smoke in the area. No sign of people. Alt. 1500.

Jack R. May-10

Noticed activity at Thompson place coming back from Aniakchak area. Noticed several people working and some clearing. Alt. 1800.
Jessie P. May-8
Two quads chasing caribou south of Egegik (about 15 mi. so.). Alt. 1500.

Ken May-14

Information from the safe mentioned business sites in Anchorage and the names of business owners. The information was divided between the team, now six members team with two more just arriving. They paired off in teams to investigate and within just a few days, the teams' meeting room was filled with photos, reports, names, histories, and any other information they had found. Several of the members met together and established a list of equipment projected to be needed for any possible operations and each member with outside reliable sources contacted their suppliers; money was sent and the gear was quickly shipped back. They did not want to be waiting for equipment.

Tony was proud of his son Eli. After all, Eli had organized his own company and was doing very well hiding his identity and all of his al-Qaeda connections. He had been at the lodge and had organized detailed plans outlining several of the sights for destruction on the pipeline. Tony remembered the rage Eli felt after hearing that their prisoner had escaped. He and six of his best trackers had gone out after the group that had rescued the lodge owner. If anyone could find them they could. But he had forgotten one important thing: the tundra environment. They were not totally equipped for the terrain. His team had come close as they watched the small plane take off the unlighted strip. He was impressed by the bold move of taking off in the dark by the pilot.

Eli had been about to start on the lodge owner to get back the papers his father had left him a week ago. They had no luck even finding a safe in the lodge and when the owner clammed up, he beat the guy to a point of thinking he was dead. That had been a few days ago and he had been on his way to the guarded shed to start again on the lodge owner just as the chopper arrived. He would wait until a later time when his father and his associates had left; he didn't want to worry them. He knew he could break the infidel with a little softening up from no food and water for a few days, plus a beating and some applied pain.

Now that the prisoner was gone, the whole cell had to move and fast. Eli had no doubt that whoever these guys were, they would be back. They sent for their helicopter support and by the time it was light, the men and equipment were all gone from the lodge. There was no alternative but to leave the attaché. Eli was furious. He would have burned the place down or used what little explosives they had left, but felt that it would push the already sparse authorities into asking for more federal help. His capture would have been imminent, having to spend more time at the lodge before there exit. He had already made a close call with the last chopper, just minutes off and away when the helicopters from the military arrived. He would get back at whoever was responsible.

There were so many places on the peninsula to hide and only a few suspected areas reported by pilots. Each had to be checked. The information was coming in quickly and Hammer pieced together some of the possible locations. One was just northwest of Katmai Mountain. The other was a bit south near the Lower Ugashik Lake. Both were areas where there had been lodges or abandoned exploratory oil sites, all vacant now. These two places showed smoke and people. They were fortunate in the fact that there were small strips throughout the whole area where a plane could be landed. Oil companies had vacated the land after unsuccessful probing. Hammer had used strips like these in the past and they would make adequate staging areas. At least the strips were flat, even if vegetation was slowly covering them. Several other areas were mentioned by pilots, but found incompatible.

Another subject of importance was brought up by Hammer. Where was that unmarked helicopter that had landed at the lodge? The helicopter had to have fuel. Hammer knew if it was out there, he or his pilot friends could find it.

The Betty B was anchored off the northwest tip of Kodiak Island, waiting for a signal from shore to pick up cargo. The crew had been selected for their experience aboard large freighters and was made up of washouts from al-Qaeda camps. No one actually washed out; they just got a different job. The captain, a raunchy looking scruffy five-foot six-inch chap, had orders to stay within range of Kodiak Island and to transport fuel and supplies to the helicopter that would land on the ship's helipad. The captain was not a patient man and being quite unattractive, the look and demeanor of a hyena, took advantage of his intimidation powers. With his yellow and brown front teeth splayed like a camel, he barked at the crew to create fear, spit flying and throwing his 220 pounds around for amusement. Displaying his nasty temperament was his way to manipulate the crew.

The ship, a makeshift fishing trawler, had worked its way from Dutch, where it had been purchased and fitted for the specific work needed without destroying its fishing appearance. The captain had been right at home in Dutch among the multinational crews and low life hangouts. He would spend most of his time nose-to-nose with the barmaids, frequenting the establishments and looking through glasses of rot gut to drown his pitiful life; it was easy to forget his religious beliefs with a bottle in one hand and a warm body in the other, hoping to find companionship for the short time they were to be in port. His first mate looked after the ship and repairs while in port.

The helicopter used by the cell was being hidden in an area just south of the Katmai range on the coastal area in a small cove off the Shelikof Strait. They covered the chopper with camouflage during the day and at night the Betty B would be its resting place. With a full load of supplies and fuel, the ship would meet the chopper at a strategic location. The chopper, an Aerospatiale Super Puma, the more modern version of Sud-Quest's original Puma, landed on the helipad for loading. The supplies were then dropped off at the training camp used by al-Qaeda. This was done right under the nose of the coast guard at Kodiak, since radar was at a premium and did not cover most of the area and the change of name and flag was easily accomplished. The ship could come and go at any time, and they did, remaining clear of known customs ports and patrolled areas.

Tony Larucci had shipments that had to go out from his warehouses. He also had several coming in. This was the way of his terrorists, always moving and never staying in the same spot. The shipments of guns to add to his stockpile and the knockoff clothes to flood the market would gain more money for his operation. His secret basement was full of arms and explosives for the pending training and operation. He felt prepared and confident.

Tony had contingency plans and a warehouse close by to use if his snitch warned of a raid. His whole warehouse could be moved in less than eight hours. This is why he never got caught; he always had a backup plan. The snitch was his ace in hand and he was confident he would never get caught.

CHAPTER 12

In Anchorage, information gathering was the order for the day and every day and night until the team was satisfied that they had enough. Hammer spent his time between the pilots and what they had seen and helping his teammates with any other tasks. The most useful was the information from the portfolios found in Bill's safe, describing stashes of weapons, warehouses, and personnel. The two-man teams spent most of their time staking out and investigating each lead. Knowing that al-Qaeda was located in their backyard, somewhere on the peninsula, the small group of men, utilizing every bit of information, organizing every ounce of paperwork and translating each word written or printed, stayed busy throughout all hours of the day and night. Hammer knew that the FBI would give anything for the information they had and yet, he felt no remorse by not letting them have it. He flew to Dillingham every other day to see the family and do menial jobs for his clients to appear busy. If the cell could find his house, he knew they were probably watching him. The girls had a week of school left before summer break and they were planning to move to Anchorage until fall. They had thought about another house on the other side of town in Dillingham, but that would be too dangerous. For safety, they would keep out of sight.

Another week had passed and a deciding point had been reached. Enough information had been compiled to send in a team to a particular area to investigate. The men were tired of the paperwork and getting anxious; they were ready to see firsthand what they were up against. The logistics of manpower would be put together by Manny and Spook, the first two team members and most competent. The two had put together the mission plans from the information as soon as it became available.

Hammer and Bill spent more time verifying credentials of each of the team. Each member of the team was scanned through several high-level computers and databases, courtesy of his friends in the air force. They had exhausted all of their resources and each of the men had come up clean. Hammer and Bill could find no evidence to connect the men to any government organization. They didn't want to spend their last twenty years in prison for violating basic laws, the same laws that the terrorists paid no attention to. Although their sources for background checks were limited, they felt they had done an adequate and thorough enough job and could now focus their time preparing for their part of the operation, not having to look over their shoulders for undercover operatives.

The group decided six members were not enough. For this operation, they would need ten men to form two teams of five. The push was started to recruit more top combat-trained and eager men. With diligence and a constant ear to the phone, calls were made and in three days they had what they needed. The idea of high wages was a major incentive and helped the recruits make up their minds.

Some of the equipment might be harder to get than Hammer had thought. His local connection would not sell automatic weapons. Both Spook and Bill had volunteered their sources and after all had been said and done, Spook was given the job of arms provider. He found a supplier who could not only provide top-quality and current weapons, but would take the larger bills that were left from the safe.

Soon, all of the team members assembled together in a motel room in Anchorage and acquainted themselves with their new team. All being combat veterans and having food and drinks supplied, the task was easy. The strategy was simple: to strangle the cell and eliminate all of the terrorists without harming civilians or interfering with the authorities. Next, Spook and Manny spoke about the logistics of the operation and informed the team when the best practical time would be for an insertion. They would assess the information in the morning, needing a fresh start, and would announce a plan at that time. Equipment was given out.

Each member was given the basics for equipment, the latest and greatest military supplies and clothes. Each of the team members had a list of their own needs that included light and specialized firearms, which Hammer seemed to have under control with his inventory from the gun safe and local suppliers. From Kevlar vests, range-finding binoculars, camouflaged clothes and boots, the team had it all. They were given new automatic weapons: MP5s with M16s for the older guys, LAWs rockets, grenades, claymores, and whatever else they needed. Both Hammer and Bill were partial to the CARs, the compact models of the M16. Two of the members, known as the twins, had their own personal weapons they had brought with them. The weapons were customized, ported, and silenced. Each team member was given a small pack with a ghillie suit.

For on-sight intelligence, the team decided that a drone would work the best. One of the team members had experience with small electrically powered silent drones and would handle that operation.

While the drone was being tested and made ready for gathering pictures, the other members were preparing by getting their weapons and equipment in perfect order and sighted in. Hammer had a friend with a private range on the outskirts of Anchorage that could be used for this task without causing any unwanted questions or suspicions. The designated five-man teams spent time getting to know in advance what was expected of them. The teams would depend on each other and their experience for backup.

There would be a point and a high man, a sniper above the point man to protect him from any unseen enemy with a lightweight large bore sniper rifle. The second team would have a 7.62 mm sniper rifle for point backup. All had radios and squad leaders were assigned for each of the two mini-teams. The two twins were specifically hired for point, one on each team.

The teams practiced movements and signals. They studied the terrain and topography, rehearsing as a team, advancing together and covering one another. They practiced night skills, camouflage skills and silent tactics, mostly to be on the same train of thought with each other. Every member was an expert at warfare and in other fields as well. They were all mostly in superb physical shape. Hammer kept track of the men in his notebook and their profile. The decided team was made up of:

Manny Sanchez: Tactics and intelligence expert with Weapons, Gulf War and classified ops, specialized in surveillance and information gathering, hand–to–hand combat expert, eastern language specialist, pilot, age 40.

Daniel "Spook" Grant: Said to be ex-CIA (unconfirmed), tactics and intelligence expert with all weapons, black ops trained, Gulf War and classified ops, specialized in surveillance and information gathering, expert supplier of equipment, age 42.

Bud Crandall: Ex-marine sergeant, expert with weapons, tactics, Gulf War, special ops, pilot, age 44.

Dave Thorp: Army ranger sergeant, expert with weapons, tactics, Gulf War, hand-to-hand expert, explosives expert, electronics expert, drone operations, pilot, age 42.

Wicky Feldman: Captain, army airborne rangers, tactics, weapons, hand-to-hand specialist, decorated in Gulf War, special ops, trained in special terrorism tactics, interrogation specialist, age 38.

James "Hacksaw" Blanchert: Ex-marine sergeant, expert with weapons, sniper; Gulf War, special ops, said to have worked for the company in Afghanistan, age 42.

Frank and Jeremy Gossamer: Army airborne rangers, expert weapons, explosives, hand-to-hand, recon, Gulf War, Iraq War, special ops, young-looking, twins, age 38.

As soon as the drone was made available, Hammer and Dave, the operator, flew the drone in the 336, a model that allowed for wing removal, and the necessary equipment to a runway near King Salmon. The two set up the drone and the equipment and tried it from the ground. Hammer was amazed with the ease of flying the aircraft and the clarity of the pictures on the computer screen from the craft. Dave demonstrated a mastery of the small aircraft and it seemed just like his flight simulator at home. When Hammer mentioned this to Dave, his reply was, "How do you think I learned how to operate the thing?" The next morning, Hammer and Dave were confident that they would get the intelligence they needed. The rest of the men flew in to King Salmon aboard Hammer's second plane and a borrowed 206 to get ready for their part.

The weather wasn't the best, but Hammer popped his head outside the motel door and observed it to be flyable. The tops, a 5,000-foot overcast with a fast-moving 3,000-foot scattered layer, light winds and rain showers, made the trip choppy to the remote strip. The intended site was located on the north end of Upper Ugshik Lake. There were a few buildings in the area that were supposedly empty. Local pilots had flown over this area and had mentioned that just recently they saw people and smoke. The area was supposed to be uninhabited. This is what the team was looking for: a location in a remote and isolated part of the peninsula that could be occupied without notice to the locals or owners of the property.

With the aid of Mount Peulik, at 4,900-feet above sea level, the drone could be operated from the northeast side and flown to the west side for pictures. The noise of the drone was their only concern, but with the wind and flying high, just under the clouds, they hoped the small aircraft would not be seen. The drone was launched and Dave, flying the electric powered drone, and Hammer flying the Skymaster took off. From the right seat of a moving plane, the control was more difficult than it might have seemed. Physical movement one way and visual movement the other was like patting one's head and rubbing the stomach at the same time. All, of course, was done in a light chop. Dave was good and it only took him a short time to get the hang of the sensation. Flying behind the hills and as high as the overcast would permit, Hammer kept in positive radio contact with the drone. The flyover by the drone was effective and the pictures were transmitted digitally back to a computer through a satellite link to King Salmon.

The drone pictures showed people at the location. The images were studied by the teams. Hammer landed the plane at the remote strip and then Dave landed the drone. They took the wings off the drone and loaded the small craft aboard 78 Bravo. The two flew back to King Salmon where they met the rest of the team and they all studied the pictures.

The drone had done its job well and both Hammer and Dave were surprised at the stealthy speed, lack of sound, and clarity of picture it produced. The analysis showed that, indeed, there were people living there and clearing the land. The silhouettes of a few figures were seen, but identifying individuals and sentry positions was difficult. The teams would move in for a "look see."

CHAPTER 13

The next morning, before daylight, the planes were loaded with men and equipment and departed. The fleet consisted of the two 336s and the borrowed 206. Four of the ten team members were pilots so flying the planes would not be a problem. The light of day was getting longer and that would be an advantage. Landing at the same strip as the scout mission had used, minimal light made for a challenge, but all were successful. The area was eerie with absolute silence, accept a slight breeze. The target site was about eight miles to the southwest, around a few hills and in knee- to waist-high brush, the scratchy nuisance type. No one complained yet, but foul words would probably be expressed before they had finished their mission.

Stealth was the concern and after last minute directions were discussed the twins were released and followed their assigned routes, one on one side of the small valley and the other on the opposite side. The sniper would follow and back the point men by establishing a higher vantage point, observing and then moving on. The three—the two points and sniper—were in full camo gear, including modified ghillie suits. The rest of the team wore camo so they were difficult to see in the brush. They all matched the surroundings perfectly. Hammer and Bill wore their old boonie hats.

The twins were in their element as they advanced through the natural terrain; no matter how harsh, they moved efficiently through the difficult water and brush. The land supported medium-height grass, mud and water and many small lakes, ponds and streams. Rocks of all sizes were there for tripping points and the clumps of low brush snagged equipment and clothes. The saw grass was merciless and if one did not pay attention and keep his hands high, the grass would cut through the skin. The temperature and wind were helpful, not too cold at near 48 degrees Fahrenheit and the whistle of the 5- to 8- mile per hour breeze concealed much of the sound of any movement.

The wildlife showed no threat from or aggression toward the team, as the unusual-looking men tried to follow whatever animal trails existed. The ten men slinked through the underbrush; the distinctive snorting and huffing noises of the animals was heard in the distant background. Most of the larger animals the men saw just kept eating and munching on the new green plants and grass of the spring growth. The herds of caribou moved quickly from one patch to another, nervously making quick movements. They chewed the low tender roots and shoots with tails flicking and ears flipping and perked, sensing, but not responding to any unusual sounds. Most were not interested in anything but food. The few brown bear that had been in the valley had moved off. A small heard of five moose, not very common this far southwest on the peninsula, were knee-high in a bog of high green grass on the shore area of a pond. They seemed uninterested in the quiet slow-moving blend of branches and leaves, the camo of the team, but continued to harvest the lush green grass from the pond floor. The animals grunted and dug, butting and playing and providing a symphony of sounds, but the men paid little attention as they struggled through the low brush.

The teams trudged on. Exasperating at times, the branches tore their clothes and tugged at their equipment. They tripped and twisted their ankles on the loose rocks. The closer the teams moved toward their target, the fewer animals were seen. That was conceived as a good sign and meant they were probably in the location they all had hoped for.

All at once, the silence was broken by one of the point men calling "Contact" through the tiny ear pieces of each man's radio. Everyone froze in a crouch and then proceeded to individually planned locations, moving to a spread position. The teams looked on and took pictures, eyeing the activity in buildings and fields. The two point men moved to a closer vantage point in a covered location and as the information came in from the pictures taken by the sniper and point men, the camp looked more and more like what they weren't looking for. There were no posted guards or lookouts. Children were playing and helping the adults gather stones from a partially cleared field. The house was small and could only hold five or six people, with the out buildings too small to lodge men or any large amounts of equipment.

A trickle of smoke came from the main house and soon the children were called in, all speaking English with no accent. The point men had long-range portable listening devices and were recording everything and listening for accents or Eastern-speaking conversation. They heard none. The decision was made to call everyone back and the teams moved to a central location, gathering behind a hill on the north side away from the small lodge. The target was not what they were looking for so they headed back to the planes, a short seven-mile walk. The teams still kept a cautious mode, one twin in front and the others in the back as they walked to the airplanes.

Hammer and especially Bill were a little out of breath by the time they reached the planes. The ten men spent little time shedding and stowing their gear in the planes. There was plenty of help and all pitched in to load. It had been a long day and they all were glad to be heading back to King Salmon and the motels.

The pictures and other information were reviewed and studied. The decision to return was a correct one, with the occupants of the small lodge never knowing that eyes and scopes were ever on them. The exercise was not a failure. Like a sports organization, the team critiqued what they had done correctly or incorrectly and would make adjustments. As any trained military person will say, a need for practice and training is the solution for any successful mission. Hammer and Bill were tired, but felt a sense of progress. At least they knew of one location that the cell would not be found. Now all they needed was the right location. Hammer was correct to not involve the FBI at this time. Better to wait and have the facts than be half right. The next day the team flew back to Anchorage.

CHAPTER 14

Mark thought he had a significant break. Facts were coming in to his office about a certain Toni Larucci, owner of a local shipping company in Anchorage with large assets and buildings that could possibly be used for the movement of arms. What Mark didn't know was that this information was tossed at him by Larucci's snitch as a tease to make him think some progress was being made by his office.

Mark sent two of his teams to the warehouse and office building for surveillance. They watched and observed, not realizing they were being set up to fail.

When Hammer and Bill got back to Anchorage, there was information waiting for them. The pilots in the region, Hammer's friends, were becoming the most valuable source of information. Another new site was starting to look good. Hammer hoped the terrain would be friendlier; he was already tired of putting ice on his ankles and knees. The team rested, repaired their equipment and their bodies in preparation for the next mission. The low brush and stout branches, along with the large rocks and uneven footing had paid a price on two of the other team members as well. They would need to tape their ankles and wear gloves the next time they entered the bush. The teams gave themselves two days to get ready for another operation. This time Hammer would make sure everyone had hard knee pads, both for support and continually falling to the knees.

Spook had found information on the location of a building in Anchorage. He and Manny had decided the scribbling on notes from the lodge had some merit and moved in to investigate. On a small square of paper in the mass of the attaché, the name Larucci and an address were faintly written in Arabic handwriting. By the time he and Manny got to the warehouse, the place had been cordoned off with yellow tape identified by the FBI in large bold letters every foot. Forensics teams were still there. They were not totally surprised to see an empty building, having the information for days from Bill's lodge safe. The cell had to have known any information left would be compromising. Spook still wanted to get inside. He and Manny would circumnavigate the two FBI teams left for surveillance and use a side door for an entrance. The front door was best left for later and with fewer agents monitoring it.

At the motel, Hammer and Bill read the latest reports from the pilots. It was now obvious that another operation was credible. The pilot reports were showing a new location of activity that seemed very unusual for that part of the mountain range. The team would be ready to move in as soon as Hammer and Dave finished the reconnaissance with the drone.

The morning arrived with stiffness for Hammer, trying to recover from the last exercise. He and Dave made the same type of trip with the drone as before. They flew the small aircraft, tucked inside the 336 to a small gravel and dirt strip some fourteen miles from a supposed abandoned lodge surrounded by several out buildings. The compound, as it had been described by the pilots, was located in a valley just northwest of the Katmai range. According to the last three reports, the pilots observed activity of "multiple persons around the buildings and fields being cleared," which they hoped the drone would verify.

Hammer and Dave used the same technique of getting the drone airborne and then controlling it from the air in the Skymaster. Dave was getting better using this technique and as the pictures came in to the members of the team from the first pass, activity was noted and before they had a chance for a second fly over, the team advised Hammer that they had seen enough and to get the drone back to keep from being compromised. The drone was landed, disassembled, stowed and Hammer and Dave were both back in King Salmon in a less than an hour.

The last plane of team members and equipment had just arrived from Anchorage and as they met together they reviewed and discussed the pictures and maps of the area. The pictures showed what they were looking for: obstacle courses, much larger lodges and buildings, target ranges, and over thirty dark complexioned men.

With the element of surprise, three to one odds were acceptable, but not what Hammer wanted. The teams that Bill and he had organized were experts and to face these kinds of odds would mean that the chances of someone getting hurt or even killed could be high. To initiate a firefight would be dangerous, besides the fact that they were not vigilantes and still had no legal right. They might not get what they were looking for: the top people. They also knew that revenge might not be as sweet if they lost even one person in their team. What would they do with thirty prisoners? The team was now ready for additional help and at four o'clock in the afternoon and with the okay of the whole team, Hammer called his FBI connection.

Hammer and Bill arranged to meet with the FBI in a few hours. The two would bring their documentation and meet at a local hotel for reasons of anonymity. The two would get there early.

Mark had finally become acclimated to the city. He had suffered through meeting after meeting, filling form after form out and getting a cauliflower ear from the conversations on the phone. He hated to be negative about the bureau, but his teams had come up with nothing of any significance that would help find and eliminate any al-Qaeda cell. The only task they had completed so far was to keep track of travel hours. He had done better than the teams himself with just the local help. Dean, his partner from St. Louis, was in Fairbanks trying to dig up information there. The other teams were all over the state. The tip on the warehouse produced nothing.

It was Sunday afternoon when he decided to check in and Mark drove to the gray building and his parking area. He pressed the gate controller and the steel chain-linked gate opened. The guard that usually tended the small shack was missing. Mark remembered not everyone worked on Sunday. He worked every day and sometimes lost track of time.

He pulled forward through the gate and it started to close automatically. Mark drove his Yukon Denali to his parking place near the elevator. Stepping out and pulling his heavy leather case to his side from the back seat, he headed for the offices. Exiting through the doors of the elevator on the third floor, he felt the vibration in his belt holster from his cell phone. It was the pilot again. *What happened now?* He answered his phone curiously and spoke for a few moments and then hung up. The pilot and his friend, the lodge owner, had asked for a meeting and he had agreed. These two were better than his teams for information and he had thoughts of recruiting them if they wanted to come onboard with the FBI. Most people would rejoice at the opportunity. For the present, he would use them for his benefit; no need to pay them.

The Larruci warehouse lay outlined by a few lights in the dark and appeared to be unattended. Spook and Manny, who had flown in with Hammer and Bill, were out of their car and heading to the side entrance. The building was located in a typical warehouse area of Anchorage, but placed at the end of a *cul-de-sac*. Being Sunday, there was no activity and only one FBI stakeout in the front. The two jimmied the lock and used low-intensity flashlights to look the place over.

It was Spook who first noticed the discrepancy in size of one of the stairways and was able to find an entrance to a hidden stairway from rub marks from a door. Climbing down a staircase, the passageway led to a large windowless basement. With a flick of the light switch, the room was illuminated, casting shadows of an interior filled with crates and wooden boxes of arms and explosives.

Manny found a larger entrance and a freight elevator by following tracks and finally a large door on wheels and rails.

As Manny looked over the inventory, Spook climbed the stairs and made a call. He soon was back in the large room and called Manny to meet him upstairs at the door they had entered from. The two met and headed back to their car, locking the door to the warehouse behind them. They stayed watching the building for fifteen minutes until a large semi-truck pulled in to the building near the hidden freight elevator. As the truck backed in, Spook and Manny left, noting the sleeping agents resting in their vehicle.

Mark walked through the lobby doors five minutes before the meeting with Hammer and Bill. He hated to be late and walked the stairway to the fifth floor. Knocking on the door, he was invited to enter, cordially greeted by the shaking of hands, followed by his customary once over of the room. He couldn't be too careful. The bed in the room was covered with pictures and maps, showing in detail a training facility and the location of an al-Qaeda camp that had been found. Mark assumed it to be overseas. Hammer made every effort not to disclose any aspect of the team in the conversation as he and Bill started briefing the agent. They had agreed to feed the agency with limited information. After all, what the Feds didn't know about the team was best for them. The agent was impressed. "You military types know how to do your jobs," was his only comment, not knowing that this was a much larger operation than just Hammer and Bill. Hammer spoke, "Bill and I need your help. We have done the recon and now we need your agency for the follow up. We have no idea when this group of terrorists will move from their present location. These pictures were taken this morning."

Again the agent was highly impressed, but still apprehensive.

The two had played their cards, but could not sell the idea to the agent. Hesitant and needing more persuasion, Hammer casually motioned Mark to a window, pointing out a tractor trailer rig with flashing lights on the street below. With a slight smugness and a swagger of confidence, Hammer called the driver and had him open the back two doors. Hammer explained that the truck was loaded with cases of arms and explosives from the warehouse that the FBI had found nothing in. Hammer would give him the truck full of weapons for help with the raid. He would even give Mark the credit for finding the camp.

In less than a minute, the agent was on the phone to his group, wanting to find out how fast he could get any of his teams together, along with any other agents in the area. Excusing himself, he stepped outside the room. In ten minutes he was back to let them know his chief had approved the operation and it would take place the following morning. Hammer acknowledged with an "Okay" and finalized with, "If we can't be of anymore help, then we will let you take it from here. Let us know how the operation went." The three shook hands and went on their way, the agent to the semi with a load of information and pictures and Hammer and Bill to the airport.

The operation was a "go" and Hammer called King Salmon to inform the teams to get ready with their plans. Hammer and Bill had placed the responsibility of the operation in the hands of the FBI where it should have been. They wanted nothing to do with prisoners and the odds they would be against. All they wanted were the top men and they would take advantage of the situation to find them. Hammer made a last call before they boarded 78 Bravo for King Salmon. "Sandy, do me a favor and come down to the hangar and pick up a sat phone. Hang out around the airport and give me a call when three choppers from across the way take off. It should be around five in the morning." She and the girls were in Anchorage staying at a hotel since school was out for the summer. She mentioned to Hammer that a little excitement might do her good. Hammer closed with, "This won't be exciting for you," and hung up.

Hammer and Bill agreed that time was at a premium and as soon as they landed at King Salmon, the four of them walked to the team's assembly room where the men were waiting. The plan was to have Hammer lead the way to the small strip and drop light sticks to mark the runway. A partial moon was out in the area providing some light. The landing would be challenging, but they picked a strip that had plenty of length. The rest of the team members were prepared for the second part of the operation. Weapons had been cleaned and equipment was checked. Last-minute words were said and the entire team headed for the planes. Hammer held Frank and Jeremy back; he wanted to speak to the two point men.

The members of the team all agreed that their operation parameters were to not interfere with FBI, but make it easy for them to take prisoners. Let the FBI do the work and get the credit.

After a short rest, the three airplanes were soon off to the small strip. Hammer, five minutes ahead, made several low runs over the runway as Bill dropped a dozen light sticks on each side of the barely visible strip. They were lucky they flew over because a small herd of caribou was grazing on the first half of the strip. There was no turn around so as soon as one airplane landed it had to be pushed to the side of the runway. When they all had landed, the planes were positioned for takeoff, one behind the other, and then covered with camouflage. As the teams made their final preparations, last minute strategies were discussed and then the point men were released, followed by two snipers, one on each side. This time, not only did the point men and snipers have ghillie suits, but the rest of the team members all carried theirs for cover near the camp.

The journey was slow and moving to the compound was tedious, very much like the last operation. Expectedly, both squads were hampered by the low scrub brush and soggy ground. The winds were about nine knots, gusting to twelve. They all were thankful that the rain had not yet started to fall. After the first two miles, the team members had to start using a heavy camo duct tape to repair the tears in their clothes. As it was, they all had to wear gloves and caps to protect themselves from the thick brush and the saw grass. The knee pads were appreciated by everyone.

Animals ignored the intrusion by the humans. The squads were made aware of any animals that might be dangerous by the point men. The sounds of bears rustling, grunting and digging in the brush, scavenging for food, could be heard all around. Fortunately, not in the direction the teams were moving. Hoofed animals grunted and grazed, thumping their feet on the rocks and hard ground looking for food. As the men continued, they noticed pairs of white swans in the small ponds. The swans would alert each other with low vocal growls to let each other know about possible danger. The teams just kept moving; they had to arrive before the FBI.

Other small animals would scamper here and there when disturbed. Shoes and socks were soaked with lots of water to walk through and navigate around. Deep, thick tundra was everywhere, making the going exasperating. Most of the time the game trails did not go in the direction the teams were heading. The point men were alert for any movement, sounds, changes of terrain and significant danger. The day was gradually growing lighter.

Four miles out from the camp, the two squads moved silently and slowly on each side of the valley, maintaining a constant speed. The animals became visible, revealed by their sounds, and seemed to be scarcer than at the start of the team's trek. At first the men could smell the animals in nearly every direction and could see many smaller ones. Now there was hardly a sign.

Expectedly, the points called a halt to the progress. According to the map, Hammer estimated that the target was still some distance away, whispering the fact to Bill. The teams moved ever so slowly to the forward positions. The point men had identified sentries in the hills just forward of their position. They had to be taken out. At that instant, Hammer received a vibration alert on his sat phone from Sandy. He answered with a whisper. She confirmed that the FBI choppers had just left. She also said, "Where are you?"

"You don't want to know," Hammer replied

"Having fun, I bet," she replied.

"Yep," Hammer said as he hung up.

Two team members volunteered to help with the sentries and were sent ahead with the point men. The snipers still remained high on the hill sides for backup. The team moved forward and, as a snake to their prey, wound through the valley, out of sight, waiting for any signal. They were still about a mile and a half or more from the compound.

A "clear" signal was given by the point men and the teams continued their movement. In time, a "Contact" was given by the points and the teams stopped as planned. Hammer had to admit that he had been impressed again by the talent and skill of the men he and Bill had assembled. The whole team, less two sentries, assembled and the point men explained a rough sketch of the camp they had made. The members gathered around and watched carefully as the point men described what they had seen.

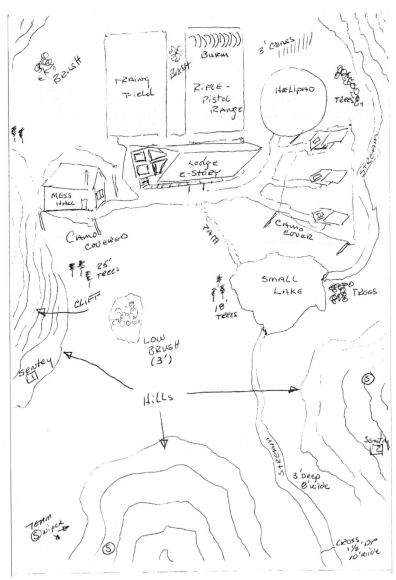

Jeremy's rough sketch of the cell camp.

CHAPTER 15

The snipers were well-hidden and on higher ground, protecting both the front for movement and the rear for the unexpected. Still early, but well-lighted, enough to see every detail of the compound, the buildings were alive with men moving here and there, performing tasks and getting ready for the day. Little did they know that soon some of them would have just enjoyed their last wakeup. The two cell sentries had been removed. Hammer and Bill hadn't seen a thing. They hadn't even seen the sentries.

Bill knew he was out of shape and older, but the rest in the past weeks and the care and nagging everyone had for him, he was able to mend and be ready for the task at hand. He still would not be able to keep up totally with the younger team members. He also still knew he was a good soldier, but after watching his team members at work, he decided that he would leave the lead and point tasks with them. Their movements and senses were at a much higher level than his and he longed for the youth he once had to compete with these youngsters. Hammer kept track of the time, estimating the arrival time of the helicopters. The whole team had dressed in their ghillie suits and proceeded toward their assigned locations; they could hardly be distinguished between the real grass and brush. They were a perfect blend and only would be detected by movement. The wind even helped them with that.

The teams moved forward for the last time. The point men called the final halt and to spread and take their places in pre-arranged positions. They all sat quietly, waiting for the FBI. This enabled Hammer to view the area and get ready for his part. They knew the snipers were above them and would not only be keeping them safe, but also be taking pictures for information.

Hammer and the rest of the team were expecting the faint "whoop" sounds of the choppers when they came, knowing the exact time of departure. They could feel the vibrations from the rotors slicing the air before any sound. That was the queue for the point men to move to the compound. In a low crouch and with their camouflage they were an exact match of the grass and ambient colors. The faint thumping of blades through the air grew louder. It was a matter of seconds before the alarm was sounded and much too late for the compound. The al-Qaeda members expected helicopter traffic, but only their own chopper. A warning had been anticipated from the sentries; fortunately they had been removed and the whole camp was now caught with their proverbial pants down. The sight of the three black, sleek-looking machines caused everyone to panic and yell, sending running bodies clamoring to find holes to hide in or weapons to fire.

The helicopters flew in fast, and as they hovered two feet above the ground, the FBI personnel jumped out covering each other. As soon as everyone was out, the helicopters flew fast and high to a prearranged location. The agents on the ground spent little time rounding up prisoners and did so like catching chickens for stew. The compound was in total disarray, with the al-Qaeda members running everywhere. The typical "drop and dash" from the choppers left little time for the terrorists to arm themselves and many just headed away from the compound with flailing arms.

Dressed in their typical black attire, with "FBI" on the back of their vests, the agents kneeled while yelling commands and firing rounds at anyone who fired at them. Crouching made for smaller targets as three groups moved toward the center of the compound, capturing and immobilizing the chaos. The terrorists, if shooting, were dropped where they stood by automatic fire. There was mostly yelling and shouting, cursing in their native tongue for being surprised and made to look like buffoons. A few shots rang out from inside the camp and several men fell to the ground. The snipers did their part, helping with leg wounds to the scampering terrorists carrying weapons. "Allah Akbar"! and other Arabic phrases were heard throughout the camp as weapons were discharged and cries of pain and surrender were given.

The FBI rounded up everyone they could without a need to fire, but some wanted martyrdom. The shooters tried to take as many of the infidels as they could, but there was no chance. A few well-placed grenades drove home the point. Meanwhile, from inside the compound, the twins had managed to move back to their original positions during all of the action. Hammer watched intently as the FBI agents drove the horde of terrorists into the center of the compound. He knew what he wanted and was in position and ready to pounce. Hammer was lucky and he knew it. He knew the opportunity he waited for would present itself, and it did.

One of the al-Qaeda members was running away from an out building toward the open brush on the far side from where the action was taking place. Unknown to him, it was only a few yards from Hammer's position. Hammer was not there by accident, just good planning by Spook and one of the twins. The location was the only place left for an escape route. The man, with a very unusual straddle to his stride hampering his speed, was tackled by a charging Hammer as he tried to run past his hiding place. Hammer caught him in a horse collar and dragged him to the ground with a thump. The terrorist, with a last effort, tried to get up, but Hammer nailed him in the ear with a right hook and he went down like a sack of sand.

Handcuffing the man with plastic ties, his feet bound and a cloth bag placed over his head, Hammer dragged him to an area of brush farther from the compound and out of sight, covering him with dead branches. He then went back to his hiding place.

The FBI had managed to apprehend over thirty al-Qaeda members with only a few injuries. One, a sprained ankle from an agent tripping over a wire to a claymore and a second, a flesh wound from a rifleman. Two of the al-Qaeda terrorists had been killed and seven were wounded.

The helicopters were called back in and stuffed with prisoners who were taken to a makeshift detention area on Kodiak Island near the Coast Guard Base. The agents scoured the buildings and retrieved a few documents and any equipment they could find. The roundtrip to Kodiak was short and after several trips from each of the large helicopters, the FBI loaded the last of their teams aboard, along with any findings, computers, paperwork or maps and pictures and headed for the base. Hammer and Bill's team had remained hidden throughout the entire operation, the FBI knowing nothing of the on-looking eyes.

As soon as the FBI was gone, half of the team headed for the airplanes. The point men retrieved their packs while Hammer and Bill made a recon pass through the buildings. They picked up their prize package, still hidden under the dead branches, on the way back to the airplane.

The teams were in good spirits and sooner or later, as they each arrived, all were glad to be back at the airstrip. The team members all greeted each other near the planes and were delighted to see everyone in good shape and no one hurt. An ice chest was waiting with drinks and there were sandwiches, courtesy of Bill. Civilian clothes were exchanged for the rags that remained of the camos. The equipment was packed in the airplanes and in turn, each plane departed for King Salmon. The day was now becoming darker under overcast skies with a light drizzle falling. However, no matter how dark Mother Nature made the day, it was bright with success in the eyes of the team members.

An hour later in King Salmon, the whole team was in great spirits and carried their bags to their motel rooms. They appeared to be just fishermen in for the season with heavy bags of equipment, not firearms. Hammer and Bill escorted the prisoner, under a heavy trench coat, to their room. The team members showered, ate, and met in Hammer and Bill's room later. The two point men each brought in separate backpacks. During the time the team cleaned up, Hammer made a courtesy call to the FBI. There had been no information in yet about the raid.

Judging by the duffle bags full of papers the twins had brought back, it appeared that once again they had the upper hand on the info from the FBI. The twins had not only found more paperwork, but another large duffle, probably full of money. Hammer and Bill left that out of sight for the moment. Out of sight was also the gimpy guy, tied up in their room, sitting in a rigged chair as uncomfortable as possible. Hammer took a picture of him and sent it to Sandy's cell phone. She replied that he was the man from the house all right, the one that had tangled with Sandy. Her only comment was, "Can he walk?"

Hammer was not sympathetic and replied, "Not very well."

He told the man that he felt sorry for him, having had to meet a tornado in such a way and also for being captured by Bill and him.

The team began organizing and translating the paperwork that had been found at the camp in one room and Bill and Hammer went to work on the duffle bag in their room. This bag was locked, but with bolt cutters it proved to be a minor setback. Similar to the first bag, but a bit bigger, they found it again crammed full of different denominations of bills. There were stacks of fifties and hundreds. The larger stacks were mostly in hundred-dollar bills. The two counted the huge amount of money and found there was near twice the total as the first case from the lodge.

The men divided the paperwork and organized it in subjects. The gist of the information indicated that the cell was still intact after departing Bill's lodge. Documentation told about most of the new camp details. The information kept the team interpreters busy for hours and soon it was obvious that they would find nothing about the head of the cell. The information and documentation was copied and bagged. The leaders were either very smart or careful not to leave any trace. That left the one and only prisoner, Mr. Gimpy, with the wide open cowboy stance.

Hammer wanted first crack at the man tied to the chair and begging in a low voice; scaring his family and killing Francis was his motive. Bill talked him out of his emotional state, siding on his own persuasive techniques and that he would take over the task. Of course, the conversation was done in front of the prisoner to make a statement and to get his blood flowing at a high rate in panic. Everyone but Bill left the room, leaving him alone with the prisoner. Bill had a few ideas, but wanted to soften the prisoner up a bit before the real work. He removed the blindfold. He began by spreading two large black garbage bags under the prisoner's chair.

Bill asked the guys next door to bring in some food and beer. Bill managed to woof down what was brought in front of the prisoner. He checked the ties and made sure they were really tight. More blood restriction. Hammer came in and motioned Bill to the porch in front of the door. Loud enough for the prisoner to hear, Hammer said to Bill, "We found all of the information we needed in the files," and turned around and left. The conversation had been prearranged so Bill went back in to the room, closing the door with no emotion. Not being given food or drink throughout the whole capture and having to walk fast to keep up or be dragged back to the planes, the prisoner was starting to shake. His heart raced from confinement, and hearing he wasn't needed anymore was about all he could take.

Bill put the blindfold back on him. The prisoner couldn't hold it anymore and his pants were suddenly wet. Bill snickered in a loud nasty tone. The prisoner's screams couldn't be heard very far through the gag and Bill hadn't even touched him yet. Hammer quietly and silently entered the room.

Bill's' next step was brutal. With two fingers like pretending to shoot someone, he placed them just below the center of the prisoner's ribs, three inches above his belly button, the solar-plex area. Bill swiftly and suddenly applied about twenty to twenty five pounds of pressure. The air could be heard gushing out of the prisoners lungs, spitting the gag out, and he went from some air to none in panic. Hammer, now silently standing behind the prisoner, simultaneously removed the pillow case and slipped a clear plastic bag over the prisoner's head, tightly squeezing it around his nose and neck. There was no air to fill the prisoner's lungs. He acted as if he had been electrocuted or hit with a Taser, showing contortions and shaking. There was minimal noise, only head twitches with no air for sound.

Bill had Hammer remove the bag after thirty seconds, slapping the prisoner's cheeks and reviving him to consciousness. Bill simply asked the question in a normal tone, "Do you have something to say?" From then on, the prisoner was a literal bundle of information. Bill had showed him just exactly what might happen if he wouldn't talk. If they had not gained the prisoner's cooperation, they were prepared to do the exercise again and again, longer and longer, until he would. This was Bill's version of a dry water board.

The prisoner was one of the higher in command and knew all of the bosses and players in the al-Qaeda cell in Anchorage. Before too much information was given out, the rest of the team was invited in and the question and answer session began. The prisoner was slightly loosened from his bonds and given food and water. When asked how he broke the prisoner so fast, Bill said, "Psychological is much better sometimes than physical. When you add a little of both, it saves time and is a lot less messy!" Hammer just smiled.

Before Hammer and Bill left for Anchorage, a strange-looking man who walked funny with plastic ties around his feet and wrists was placed at the front gate of the Air Force base, along with a fully packed duffle bag of papers and documents. Hammer gave his friend, the commanding officer, a call, telling him where the information and prisoner were and to come and collect the garbage. The MPs arrived quickly as Hammer and Bill watched from a distance. The CO was overjoyed with the information. Hammer also told him that this was the man who broke into his house and put his family in danger. The CO was quite pleased he had what the FBI didn't. Eventually the CO received a commendation from his superiors for his actions. Hammer knew how to win points.

That day, the whole team flew to Anchorage and for their last task asked to investigate the business of Tony Larucci for any additional information. Spook knew anything left was all gone by now, but played along anyway. They found an empty building. Nothing was left, not even the furniture.

At the team meeting in the afternoon, each member was given money with a bonus and a plane ticket, and then the team disbanded.

CHAPTER 16

Mark sat back in his chair wondering how he had the good fortune of meeting two men who had volunteered information his agency should have been able to obtain, but didn't. That's what his department was supposed to do. He wasn't going to complain, mind you, except to his teams; he just accepted the fact that the operation, eliminating the cell, was very successful thanks to the civilians. The prisoners were not extremely knowledgeable and there was not a lot of information in the al-Qaeda compound. One unusual comment by two of the more experienced agents was that they thought they had been watched throughout the entire operation. Mark replied, "Maybe so, but by whom?" They just replied by saying they didn't know. It was just a feeling.

Mark had leads for an investigation of another of Larucci's companies in Anchorage that was listed in some of the confiscated documents from the compound. He sent two teams to investigate the buildings mentioned and both were found to be empty. Up to this point, Mark realized that every building his unit had searched had been empty. Like the rest of the other information his teams came up with, the trail led to nothing and resulted in a dead-end. The situation in Anchorage looked suspiciously like St. Louis. Mark called his teams in and had them do some constructive work: file their field reports on the computer. He had reached his limit doing their jobs.

The day the terrorist compound was taken was a bleak one for some. The money, information, and equipment, along with the personnel the FBI captured, was enormously important to operation Caribou. There would be no operation without the operatives. The Betty B still remained off the coast of Kodiak Island. With the shipping lanes being patrolled as they were normally, leads and information from captured prisoners gave way the facts that a ship and a helicopter had been used for transporting supplies and personnel into the compound. The helicopter would approach and depart to the south. That's where the coast guard search intensified.

She lay low in the inlets of Kodiak Island on the west side, working her way south at night. Unfortunately for her, that's when the coast guard made the most effort to locate and track ship movement. On the fourth day, as the ship crossed the Shelikof Strait, a patrol helicopter spotted the moving vessel. The chopper pilot made a radio call to his base on the island and the base relayed a message stating the coordinates to two coast guard vessels at the southern tip of the island.

The race was on and having no place to hide, the coast guard intercepted the Betty B after a high-speed chase of twenty knots and the aid of a helicopter, the door gunner being extremely persuasive. The ship was boarded and searched and then taken over by coast guard crewmen. They proceeded to the base on Kodiak Island where one of the FBI teams and base coast guard personnel searched the ship for contraband and any other illegal items not on the manifest.

The search produced numerous barrels of jet aircraft fuel, crates of food and clothes, a few illegal weapons, which the captain had said they needed for sea pirates, and some machinery. The weapons were confiscated and the ship was sent on its way. The coast guard knew something was wrong, but could not prove it, so the Betty B headed for Dutch and then the 200-mile limit. As long as they were out of the area the Coast Guard had solved the problem.

The helicopter used to supply the camp rested near the shoreline on a makeshift platform and was covered by a camouflaged canvas. The crew was nearby, hidden in a small hut with a sod roof of native vegetation that made it almost impossible to see. More information from the prisoners proved helpful and indicated the exact direction in which the helicopter always came from and flew to. Since aircraft flights were at a minimum in that area, the coast guard sent out more patrols. The first week was in difficult flying conditions, with bad weather. The next week, however, was much more productive with help from wind gusts displacing the tarp and exposing most of the tail section and rotor of the chopper. The pilot and crew, hearing the coast guard helicopter overhead, made a mad dash for the underbrush and were apprehended trying to escape. The four were caught easily in the scrub brush, complaining of pain and discomfort from being tangled and cut from the snagging brush and saw grass.

The coast guard brought a qualified pilot in to fly the chopper out and they kept it in a hangar at Kodiak. Months went by and no one claimed the machine. The Coast Guard, not wanting to have the machine just sit, asked for volunteers to put it in to good condition and when the chopper was mechanically sound, a coat of paint was added as the finishing touches. The men of the base donated the paint. The big beautiful helicopter was then sent to the Anchorage hospital for medical use and emergencies.

Having such bad luck with his attempts at causing havoc, one would assume Larucci would have left the area, but he was only made angrier and extremely upset with the loss of the equipment from his warehouse and training camps. He had buyers and had planned shipments for all of the arms and explosives that had been in the basement of the warehouse. Al-Qaeda bosses would be extremely disappointed again with his hard luck. He only hoped that they would understand. No matter what the circumstances, he would get even; after all, Anchorage was not the only city vulnerable in Alaska and there was always the possibility of training his men in Canada.

Hammer and Bill had an enormous collection of equipment and stored it in a container unit near the airport in Anchorage. Hammer gave a couple of his prize hand guns to two of the members of the team who were overjoyed with the hard-to-find, exceptionally fine specimens. He figured these pieces of his collection would be better off in the hands of experts than just sitting around in the storage unit. He had emptied his gun safe for the team's requirements, but now had an arsenal of more than imaginable modern weapons stored in the container.

Needless to say, their team had been impressive. They had succeeded in every aspect of the planned operation. Their heads should have been held high, but the fact of not being able to find and capture Larucci was discouraging. The collection of information was boxed and also stored in the storage unit. There were six boxes of information including pictures, documentation, receipts, memos, and personal notes. Hammer and Bill hoped this would be the last of the al-Qaeda cell and that they had made it clear there was no room for terrorists on US soil. Alaska and the rest of the states had no room for Larucci. At least that's what they hoped for. Their intuitions and experience should have helped place any outcome in doubt. With all of their savvy, they knew that when dealing with fanatics like this group, there was always a possibility of repercussions.

Bill's lodge was the most important thing to him now. He spent time hiring a new cook and wife combination to help run the place. For security, a retired friend of one of the team members was hired. The new security man also loved to fish and was used for a guide when Bill wanted to stay close to the lodge. The big beautiful lodge had been cleaned and made bigger and more beautiful in the next several months and the clientele was back eating and fishing to their hearts' content. After all, this part of the country supported some of the best lake and stream fishing in the world. Bill was content with his business, but lonesome.

He replaced his two dogs with two litter mates from a standard poodle-golden retriever mix out of Seattle. His joy was to sit on the front porch of his lodge with the puff balls of fur in his lap, enjoying the view of Lake Iliamna and sipping a Corona. His health kept getting worse after that beating he took from the cell members. Bill's mind wasn't nearly as sharp and he definitely had physical damage after being beaten, at least once to unconsciousness.

Hammer thought of nothing but his family and business. When they all moved back to Dillingham from Anchorage, the girls would not move back into the old house, no matter how hard Hammer tried to convince them it was safe. They purchased a house on the opposite side of town. This one was not so secluded and they had neighbors.

Hammer, now with two planes flying, decided to send 78 Bravo down to British Columbia to have it painted. Meanwhile, he rented a second plane, the 206 they had used for their team transportation. New engines were put on 78 Bravo before the new paint. He worked hard during his spare time installing new engines with new lord mounts, new hoses, new hardware and all new exhaust. Eventually, between flying and family, with the help of another mechanic, he completed the work. In two months, 78 Bravo was painted and the whole family went down to Vancouver for a holiday and to pick it up. It was a fun trip, but cut short due to the booming business back home.

Hammer worked hard and at this point of his increasing business, had to think about hiring another pilot. Out of 300 applicants, he found a recently retired air force major with a commercial certificate who loved the area. She would need a little training, but her attitude was what he was looking for. She would also have to get a 135 air taxi check ride for VFR before she could earn money. Hammer was still a great instructor and had agreed to work with her.

During the summer months and the finish of salmon season, the flying business was booming. Katie, the new pilot, had passed her 135 check ride the first try and would fly the freight. One of the planes had the seats removed and could haul a fair amount. Hammer would fly passengers. When Katie had enough hours, she could carry passengers, but she had to qualify for the company insurance minimums by accruing Alaska flight time. Hammer had to service the lodge almost every day, which kept him busy.

Katie, being an ex-major in the air force, was by now a loner. She had never married due to the competitive person she was. She was like Sandy in the fact that she liked the martial arts. She loved to swim, jog, and hike. Her expertise was computers. She had files after files of the photos she shot of the local area on her laptop. Flying had been her hobby. At a height of 5 feet, 10 inches, she had played team sports at Stanford. Not much of a girly girl, she was still feminine. She knew her current events and was even up on the Academy Awards and latest dance steps. Her last station was McChord Air Force Base in Tacoma, Washington where she ran the air traffic control.

A cat person, although she loved any animal, she was a fanatic for a good game of touch football. Her favorite pastime was hiking the Olympic Mountains, the range between the Puget Sound and the Pacific Ocean. Fishing was not her thing because she had to be busy. At fifty-two, she seemed forty and always looked for challenges. She left the air force because she had the chance to retire and move on to new challenges.

The summer was coming to a close and Hammer flew as many hours as he could. The family activities seemed to fill whatever time was left, making the summer break seem short. For the girls, school started again and Sandy was back at her job. Replacing Francis was hard, but seeing Bill's little pups gave Hammer the idea that if he got two for his girls, that might raise their spirits. By the time Hammer had made arrangements, all of the pups were spoken for except the runt of the litter and a sister. He didn't care. They would be loved no matter what. When the pups arrived from Seattle, the girls were overjoyed, squealing and hugging them, tossing toys and watching their big feet and clumsy bodies tripping and playing awkwardly, trying to outdo each other or be the first to the thrown toy. The girls' attitudes improved in a week. The pups helped make them all forget what happened in the past year. It might have been only temporary, but the joy the pups provided brought the entire family back together.

CHAPTER 17

Throughout the ordeal of planning and completing the teams' operations, something had been bothering Hammer. How was it possible that the top people of the al-Qaeda cell were never caught? And how come the FBI had not gotten back to either Bill or himself with at least a thanks or any information at all?

Hammer pondered these and other unanswered questions for months. Spook had once told him that, "Some particular events didn't figure," and to "not take chances," a meaning that was not evident at the time. Hammer never took chances if he didn't have to. He figured his luck had been used up in 'nam. Maybe luck wasn't the word, rather the calculation of risk and making an effort to know an opponent or the situation, preempting luck, a philosophy fliers used. Pilots in this region did not count on luck. Maybe that's what Spook meant, that the game wasn't over. The beast with the brains was still out there. According to the last set of files seized, the cell was going ahead with an attack on the air force base, the pipeline and the food sources. The times and dates had been left undisclosed.

Hammer and Bill would make time to discuss current events at the lodge. Meetings became more frequent, having had no response from the feds, and soon they met biweekly. It was relatively convenient since customers and supplies were coming in almost daily. Bill was in a remote area and he and Hammer both knew how vulnerable the lodge was; after all, there still could be a kind of vendetta for the past actions. Hammer continually worried about Bill and the health of his friend. Local doctors had given him a checkup, but as stubborn as he was, Bill refused to take advice and go to Anchorage for more tests; saying that he felt fine and had no long-lasting effects from the past beatings. This was not entirely true at all and unknown to Hammer; several of Bill's bodily systems were beyond repair and beginning to deteriorate. Time would be the deciding factor.

The FBI left Hammer and Bill out of the informational loop. Informing them of any new or important findings concerning danger or threats to either one of them was just not going to happen. As long as Larucci and his thugs were alive, the facts remained that the two would most likely always be hunted. They also knew that the chances of staying alive would diminish as the cell was given time to relocate and grow strong again.

The money that was found during the encounters with the cell was almost all laundered and in several accounts. Hammer's intuition was to use that money to find information and keep from being bullied, something he hated most of all. The terrorist had implanted the thought of being vulnerable in his mind. His thoughts were mostly of how to keep the cell away from his family. The terrorists had done their job well. The FBI was no help. The local authorities had their hands tied with budget cuts and just trying to patrol the cities and areas the majority of the population needed. This left only one feasible course of action: go after the cell himself. Short of a full year since the last encounter, Hammer knew he would have to start the search for information from scratch.

As Hammer recalled, at the last meeting with the authorities, speaking about the FBI, the speculation was that the cell would not be after them and its focus would be on organizing other training camps or facilities, probably out of state. If that was the case, how come Hammer's mind was not at ease? Bill and he surmised that they could no longer take chances. They had already left the questions they were asking unanswered too long and a backup plan was well overdue. Hammer was tired of having to look over his shoulder all the time, questioning everyone and not knowing if there would be someone waiting for a clear shot at him or his family.

Jackie, at almost sixteen, was the light in her father's eye and developing into a beautiful young lady. She was now a sophomore at the high school where she played soccer and volleyball. Her favorite of all was a tendency toward the boys. Amanda, on the other hand, was eleven and going on sixteen. She saw all of the activities and fun her sister was having and wanted to be a part of them. Amanda was still in ballet and dance, but her emphasis was being Sandy's student in martial arts.

Amanda had a gift and a shelf full of trophies to prove it. She won several martial arts competitions and tournament events in Anchorage. Sandy had wanted to go to a couple of the larger tournaments in the Seattle area, but Hammer had told her to wait a few more years, fearing recognition from al-Qaeda. At her age, she participated in the young adult, sixteen-year-old level. Some of her trophies were at the adult level. Sandy and Amanda certainly had a bond.

The schools were good in Dillingham and like most in Alaska, built with oil money. Sandy was able to drive the girls to school, having the convenience of her office just a few blocks away. Her job called for statewide travel, if there was a need. Hammer's work was busy and most of the time, Katie, loving the air time as she did, flew the planes while he worked on the repairs and took care of the girls. He spent as much time as was needed on the planes and flying, but always had that paranoia of being out of control with the situation. Katie was getting plenty of hours and could now haul everything including people. The airplanes were shiny with new paint and both had strong, low-time engines. Hammer's love was still flying and the challenges of being a bush pilot in Alaska. Being the best at what he did was the only feeling keeping him sane and working.

The family house was much nicer than the older home, being only five years old. The trade off for the view, the ocean and the wild life, was missed. One of the advantages of the new house was that each member of the family had his or her own room. Jackie had a sports and rock theme, with large pictures of Mia Hamm and Sue Bird being the focal point. Hannah Montana was in there someplace. Amanda had her own ideas for decorations. She had the nature pictures, including polar bears and whales, with a large picture of Chuck Norris as Lone Wolf McQuade.

Hammer had a habit of spoiling the girls and would take them to Anchorage to shop, see a new movie or eat at one of the restaurants during the weekends. They were growing fast and he didn't want to miss any of it.

Images would suddenly appear in Hammer's mind, such as coming home to a dark house with lights off and two bodies lying on the floor, not knowing if his family was among them. The unforgotten impressions of seeing that pile of fur that was once a companion and part of the family ate away at his insides and caused more hostility. He wasn't the only one on constant alert, threatened and continually suspecting everyone unfamiliar they saw as a possible danger. Sandy had the visualization of the brutality the cell had implanted in her mind, too, with the thoughts of mental images of death and the threat to the girls.

Hammer knew the name of the top man, Larucci. No matter how hard he tried, and he tried diligently every night, he could not get any pictures or information about the man and his heartless thugs. He knew of the warehouse and of the equipment they had taken. Much of it, less the small part the FBI was given, was still stashed in the container at Anchorage International.

Hammer would get angry not knowing the location of Larucci. As long as he was on the loose, there would always be that feeling of living in danger. One afternoon, while talking with Bill, they both agreed that they had reached a point of wanting to do something. Both were tired of running on little sleep and reacting to the smallest of sound. Larucci and his people had the time to reorganize and the authorities were doing nothing. The evil and dangerous cell had to be eliminated, no matter what the cost.

Mark had been pleased with the results of the raid: the capture, imprisonment, and questioning of the members of the al-Qaeda cell. Since the raid, the unit's time had been spent mostly on this project and inspecting seized equipment and men. His teams interrogated the prisoners, getting information and compiling computer and hardcopy files of the cell's activity. When finished, each member of the cell was sent to San Diego and other military prisons. His only disappointment, as was Hammer's, was not apprehending the head personnel. He didn't think much of the size and strength of the cell because of the small amount of equipment they had confiscated and lack of written information gathered in the camp. He was, however, pleased with the split-second timing and coordination his teams had demonstrated to catch the terrorists, totally unaware as they had.

Mark had no knowledge of the money and information found by Hammer's team and as far as he was concerned, this was the end of what he was brought here to do. Mark was satisfied with just accepting praise for the ability to make good decisions resulting in the actions of his unit and their quest to gather necessary and accurate facts. Never was there mention of civilian help. Kudos were given to Mark and his unit and the beginning of a few shovels full of dirt were added to help fill that deep hole of Mark's. Maybe he would get to California after all. He didn't care about any civilian problems, only *his* desires.

In the afternoon a few days later, following the decision to start a new search, Hammer, with a plan, contacted Bill and then headed for the airport. As he walked by Katie, working on one of the planes in the hangar, he muttered, "Handle it, I'll be back," and climbed in to 78 Bravo. He took off and headed directly to the south end of Lake Iliamna, hoping that Bill would help shed some light on his thoughts and strategies, possibly adding a little insight of his own.

At the lodge, the two sat on the porch overlooking the lake and talked. Bill had a scrunched-up face as he listened to an article Hammer had just finished reading. "FBI teams brought about the capture and confiscation of al-Qaeda personnel and equipment." Hammer read the last paragraph as quoted by the unit leader of the special FBI unit. Bill commented that, "This Mark somebody really had everyone fooled." Hammer agreed and suggested that they were now on their own again. Bill was both disgusted and shaking his head in a gesture of agreement; he would just rather use a more forward approach and more aggressive tactic like smacking the guy upside the head.

Understanding Bill's "charging head on" methods, he began to get some positive feedback and the two came up with a usable plan. Obviously, they had no faith in the FBI and who could blame them? After all, the two men had done quite well on their own, except for one small problem. Larrucci was still on the loose. Bill snickered when Hammer read about the FBI's ability to solve cases as written in the local paper.

Was Al-Qaeda really through in this area like the FBI had said in the article? They both knew it was not and there was still a threat to try and blow up the pipeline and raise havoc in the state if they weren't stopped. Al-Qaeda would not forget what the two of them had already done. The top members would seek out some sort of revenge and, if successful, cause more destruction to even more people. Hammer's Vietnam experiences might have been placed in the back of his mind, but he was still reminded of right from wrong. Terrorism had been wrong then and it was most certainly wrong for al-Qaeda and their society of blood-thirsty terrorists to be on U.S. soil anywhere.

More talking, waiting for something to happen to them was not going to happen. It was again up to them for action. No more waiting and no more procrastination. This would just lead to their demise. He would contact Spook when he returned to the hangar. Complete elimination would be the only way to beat the cell. Legal or not, help or not, the only way to handle this situation was to reestablish the team. They would use the law of the frontier, a law of their own. How much did al-Qaeda still know about them? Hammer would take precautions.

After an agreement, the two decided on Dillinghan as the best place for their preparation and planning. Silent was the tone, as the two rode the lodge's John Deere "Gator" to the airstrip. At the runway the plane was given a quick walk-around and after a handshake Hammer climbed in and fired her up. He took off and went direct to Dillingham and his hangar. The other airplane was out, so he taxied to the side of the main door and shut 78 B down; he made a bee line to the office and pulled out his wallet. He rummaged through the cards he kept and pulled out one particular card he had hoped he would never have to use again. Dialing the number, he waited for a couple of rings and after the third ring, a voice said, "Hello!"

"Spook, this is Hammer," he said. "We have another problem." Briefly, the two talked about the situation and they agreed on a meeting place and time.

Hammer continually looked for clues and information, using what time he had before the meeting with Spook. The week before, he had told Bill he had spent a night in Dutch Harbor with a friend. He had a late flight in and rather than fly back to Dillingham at night, he stayed in Dutch at a motel. During that stay he heard a name that sent chills down his back. Evidently, a company called Lucci was working out of Fairbanks and shipping parts to and from Dutch Harbor. Hammer poked around the different freight-receiving offices and found that the ferry office knew the name well and had been doing business for several months with the company. He found that crates of machinery were being sent from a company in Seattle through Dutch to the Lucci Company in Fairbanks. On occasion, the Lucci Company would send shipments back to Seattle. Hammer didn't know if the name was coincidental or Larucci was trying for the "smug of the year" award. He jotted down the address in Fairbanks.

Hammer and Bill met Spook at the Clarion. They exchanged greetings and began to fill him in with their concerns. Hammer had stopped at the storage unit and picked up a few items, including the boxes of documents and a couple of side arms. Spook was appreciative and thanked them, stating that the information would be a good start, but not to be too impatient. He hadn't realized just how much sensitive paperwork the twins had taken from the compound. "No wonder the FBI had been disillusioned with the lack of information left by the cell," he stated.

They also filled him in with the news about a Lucci Company out of Fairbanks. Spook would look into the company and any leads that might come his way. He asked Hammer if he could have another team member and it was agreed upon. Backup was important for observation and stakeouts. Hammer handed Spook a credit card and $10,000 in $50 bills for expenses. Spook only had one other question: "Did the FBI ever call you back?" Hammer's answer was simple and quick as they left: "Nope."

Hammer was possessed with a demon in his head; that demon was Larucci. Everything he did was fueled by the thoughts of catching the man. Now that he had the name, he needed a face to go along with it. He couldn't always rely on Bill and having to fly to the lodge for possible identification. The task of finding what he needed would be just a matter of patient research, as before. He needed a break finding Larucci and prying him out from the rock under which was hiding. Hammer's motives were simple: to give Spook the advantage of knowing the hiding place. He was actually *competing* to find the head of the cell. He was not necessarily competing with anyone else or the FBI, just with time.

Hammer's only source of information was his Mac computer located in an upper den in the house. The room was like a small cave, keeping him isolated, without distraction. Being dark, except for the light from the twenty-inch screen, helped with his focus and being alone he could concentrate on the smallest details. He stroked and soothed the keys, using several search engines to compile facts. He usually consumed a half dozen Red Bulls and two or three boxes of cupcakes in the small refrigerator to help stay awake.

Companies with warehouses in Fairbanks were what he was mainly searching for, hoping for any connection with the sound-alike names and owners possibly paired as father and son. Company after company appeared on his small screen. Little did he know that what he was after was right under his nose.

One evening, Hammer just so happened to hit the correct keys and an article came up featuring a father of about fifty-years-old and son who was twenty-two. Their names were not shown under the picture, but a banner on the building behind them gave the name "The Larucci Co." The company building was registered under an entirely different name and was being listed as a recently established marine parts business in Fairbanks. The article stated that the company was new, which did not gel with the source in Dutch. If this was actually the Larucci Hammer was looking for, he was amazed at the amount of fortitude he continued to show, his arm over the shoulder of his son in the picture. Would Larucci knowingly put his face on the Internet on purpose? Was he daring Hammer or the FBI? Did he even know Hammer? Could this company actually be father and son? If so, did the father and son duo believe they would never be caught being so close to Anchorage, or was that the point? Were they so unafraid of the authorities? Whatever the reason, it made Hammer want to head for Fairbanks with his .45-70. It would do no good though; he had to be smarter than the father and son. He had to outmaneuver the pair, rather than let them slip away again. There would be no law involved. He and Bill would not lose the leaders a second time. This was the last chance to eliminate the leader and be free.

Hammer spent hours following up on leads and decided to share what he had found with Spook. He explained how he tracked Larucci and his company through the secretary of state and licenses to find other owners of reference and found a parent company out of Seattle. Going to the parent company and then the secretary of state in Washington, Hammer found several names as controlling officers of different companies, one being Larucci. There were no pictures so he kept looking, searching for any description of the men he sought. The picture he had found from the paper was nondescript and distorted and would not work for identification.

At three in the morning, and after three days of searching, he hit pay dirt again—he found a dedication picture of the board of directors for a company out of Seattle. The company was the Crown Corporation, dealers in heavy equipment. They seem to pop up more frequently and might have the roots to more than just one cell. Right clicking and saving the picture to e-mail, Hammer sent it directly to Bill. Spook said, "I thought I was supposed to do the investigation", but continued to listen. Hammer went on with his findings. It wasn't until eight the next morning that he heard from Bill.

Hammer lazily rolled over on the couch at the sound of a delivered e-mail, swung his feet to the floor and sat at his computer. Moving the mouse to activate the sleeping screen, he clicked on the message and read the response. Bill was glad to hear from Hammer and hoped that the plan was going well. He read the remainder of the massage and studied the picture. Bill had replied with his normal few simple words and had typed, "They were both there."

Spook scanned the pictures he had been sent and placed them in a file. He let Hammer know that he would start on the leads in Fairbanks the next day. Manny, Spook's requested partner, would soon be in town to help and they would call for a meeting when they had information.

In two days, with all of Hammer's help and an abundance of coffee and donuts, Spook and Manny observed the office building and warehouses owned by the Larru Co., once the Pacific Northern Marine Co. They gathered information including pictures, routines, and vocal sounds for identification, using the most advanced technology. By the end of the week, Spook called Hammer and Bill to set up a time in Anchorage to meet. The main intent of the meeting was to exchange information, and according to Spook, his stakeouts revealed a need for immediate action. Recordings from conversations of the employees and supervisors revealed that *time was at a premium and they needed to act soon.*

CHAPTER 18

The weather wasn't particularly good Saturday and the girls were doing school work in a sassy mood. Sandy was the main target and they wanted to be taken shopping. Hammer let Katie do the flying for the day and he left for the lodge to pick up Bill early in a windy, cloudy, and rainy overcast. Sticking to an altitude of 200 feet above Nushagak Bay and around the point to Kvichak Bay toward King Salmon, the ceiling rose to between 800 and 1,000 feet. Hammer followed the Kvichak River to the lake and landed at the lodge. Bill was ready and said his goodbyes to the guests, taking orders for items from stores in Anchorage.

He and Hammer took off and headed for Big Mountain and the lowlands at Kakhonak, taking a left turn at Kamishak Bay. From there, the sky opened up and they flew around Augustine Island, north of Kenai, and then landed at Anchorage International. Hammer tied the plane down and they both climbed into the Yukon Denali, the company car at the hangar, and headed for the hotel. They met Spook and Manny at the Clarion, located at the east end of Lake Hood, and talked about what they had found and a plan of action.

Spook had found the location of the holdings in Fairbanks and confirmed that it consisted of an office building and two smaller warehouses. They would have to continue surveillance and establish schedules to assure reliability for any aggressive action. They didn't want to be surprised by overwhelming odds or lose the players they were all after. Bill had nothing to say and Hammer only hinted that this might be a job for the FBI, thinking about possible injuries against a larger force. Spook shook his head, insisting that the FBI might cooperate, but it was highly unlikely. "Would we all settle for the outcome of being kept in the dark as to what really happened, and who actually gets captured or killed?" Spook asked.

The bureau really didn't have to tell them anything, but courtesy dictated some kind of answers, whether truthful or not. The tone of the meeting was hostile; they were all tired and short-tempered. The final decision was to leave the FBI out of the picture completely. Hammer thought he might have hurt Spook's feelings with his statements and, backing off for the moment, showed him respect by agreeing. He also gave him the go ahead for whatever he needed. Spook had been reliable in the past.

Spook indicated he needed more listening devices and could pick them up downtown on the way to the stakeout. Hammer and Bill had chores of their own to do in town to finish their business and both, realizing that the tension would only increase, dismissed themselves and headed for the truck. Bill and he were getting anxious and impatient. The slow pace of stakeouts took valuable time and, along with the need for another few days and maybe as long as a week, offered no relief from the stress the two were feeling. They headed for the Tea Leaf. Spook and Manny prepared for a few more long days and nights in Fairbanks.

A few days turned into four and then a full week before the call came from Spook, indicating that he and Manny had gathered what they were looking for, reliable places and times the cell leaders frequented the buildings. Hammer was reaching his limit for waiting. He hated the thought of these terrorists slinking secretly around their cities right under their noses. Where was the FBI? He had always been a fighter, seeking the right way, the "Dudley Do-Right" attitude and usually cheering for the underdog. Now, as in the past weeks, he was constantly looking behind himself or pressing the girls to move faster to enter the car or hustle to walk through the front door of the house for safety. He had created a habit of speaking under his breath and to no one in particular. The subject was mostly about the time it was taking for the stakeout and this whole process. Larucci could have moved or relocated; the chase was getting timely. He was showing his frustrations and getting short-tempered with everyone, including Spook. If his team was not successful, they might never be able to live a normal life again. He was losing control, the one thing pilots can't live with. The vulnerability of his family continually flashed in his mind, another thought he had no control of; it pictured him helpless to confront his once faceless threat. Patience was difficult.

Hammer was always thinking about the legality of any operation, which, as it was at Katmei, had the possibility of his team getting caught by the authorities; having to explain their presence and in possession of automatic weapons. The head of the FBI unit always had that attitude that "Civilians always wanted to butt into our business." In actuality, the FBI was being spoon-fed, considering that they were doing nothing to find and catch Larucci. What was more criminal, going after Larucci or not doing anything to find the terrorists? He would not give up now and had no doubt that as long as the leaders were free, there would be a probability of more camps. The cell leaders and their support had to be eliminated; they would only find another source of money to replace what was taken from their camps. Hammer slapped himself back to reality. They had current information and they needed to act now or the trail would only get cold. They may never have another chance to take down the cell. He rushed to the plane.

Information obtained from the past week was shared during the second meeting and the facts confirmed that the four of them could not complete an operation of three buildings and heaven knows how many men. The personnel were always changing. Either a larger team had to be reassembled or they needed to bring in the FBI. This was not what Hammer had hoped for. Again his mood turned cynical.

"It would take just too long to assemble a team", Spook had said. Hammer hesitated in a huff, impatiently searching for a card in his wallet, one he used before. Scrounging for the card gave him more time to calm himself and think about what he was going to say. The ritual of dialing and speaking to the agent was beginning to make him more uneasy, having once said before, "This was the last time." A half-hearted voice on the other end greeted him with a sterile, unemotional tone; a voice of a person not ready for an interruption of work at this time. Not really in a good frame of mind, Hammer stressed the importance of a meeting and the exchange of new information with the agent.

Within an hour, the agent appeared at the door of Hammer's room and, with the shake of hands, entered and listened as Hammer reviewed the information about the company in Fairbanks. Bill glared at the presentation, remaining in the background. Spook and Manny were watching from the room next door with a miniature camera in the room and the screen on their laptop.

Hammer was blunt at first and asked about the last operation—what was found and why the secrecy. The agent was not going to divulge any particular specifics, but gave them an overall synopsis. He started out by explaining that the FBI did not get much information from the camp, but did from the interrogation process. The agent continued by giving them a prearranged packet of information. Hammer interpreted this as a gesture of good faith, but he had no faith in the FBI. The information was useless, considering that Hammer already had what he was given and much more.

He was starting to get annoyed knowing that the FBI agent was manipulating him. Thinking of taking his frustrations out on someone, he realized that an FBI agent probably was not the best choice. Task at hand and slowly relieving his desire to smack the agent, he thought about the packet he had been handed. The information was a tease to show good faith, but instead showed the agent's lack of knowledge and poor judgment.

The agent spent about ten minutes reading the well-laid out material Hammer had handed him and then looked up at Hammer, "I'm impressed. Do you guys need jobs?"

Hammer's response was, "You say that every time we meet. What's wrong with your unit?" He gave a half-smile, half-smirk.

Hammer and Bill chuckled and then Hammer asked if they were interested in discussing any action. The agent's reaction was, "Sure, let's put an end to this."

Hammer constantly questioned the past actions of the agency, having very little confidence in the ability of the unit. He explained what exactly the al-Qaeda cell was planning and the possibility of retribution to both his family and to Bill and his property. "There has to be something done," Hammer concluded. This was the motive for their work. He needed assurance that there would be an exchange of information this time when the whole thing was finished.

The company's employees should be arrested now while the intelligence was fresh and accurate. The top men will be there and this will be the final chance. The FBI agent agreed and told them he would initiate a fact-finding mission and commence preparation for an operation at once. The only request from Hammer at the closing was to reveal any information the cell might have about his family or Bill. Hammer felt relieved and that this meeting was hopefully a start to a happy ending to their problems. Maybe the months of worry and frustration would come to an end. Although he felt relief, having given the FBI enough to conduct a raid, he still could not trust the bureau, and his experience told him to beware and not to place much faith in their abilities.

The plan was simple, to simultaneously take over the two warehouses and one office building. The most opportune time to start observing was midmorning, giving the employees a chance to be at work, including the top personnel. The short time of surveillance by the FBI had proved Hammer's team to be correct and that the top people usually showed up around that time.

The signal to begin the raid was given by Mark and the FBI teams moved in, breaking down doors and capturing twelve men and women who worked for the company. The warehouses revealed a number of arms and expensive items for trade. Two of the six captured from one of the smaller warehouses resisted and were killed. According to the prisoners, Darby and Chuck were the two. They would never surrender to infidels, as the commencement of weapons firing and the traditional shouting of "Allah Akbar", followed by the echo of repetitive gunfire, a hail of bullets in all directions and then silence. Mutilated and torn bodies were all that was left of the terrorists. The FBI loaded large paneled trucks full of the contraband, leaving just a few crates of actual boat parts.

The office building contained mostly business documents and a small staff of hardworking employees who knew nothing of the underlying company. The only thing that was missing was the person they had been after. Where he was no one knew. There was also a company safe that needed to be opened. It was small enough that the FBI took it with them.

Mark Glenrose, team leader, wrote a report on the raid.

1. *The FBI teams worked diligently gathering a great deal of information for their raid on three buildings. The unit's teams supplied accurately detailed information. FBI stakeouts collected and organized informative files detailing timelines, known felons and people of interest. The personnel and their routines were observed and an action was planned. The results of the raid produced many prisoners for questioning and a large inventory of arms and equipment. These weapons would have been undoubtedly used against the United States.*

2. *The information gained from the raid gave names, inventories and locations of warehouses, offices, safe houses, sponsors and top operatives in the al-Qaeda cell located in Alaska and in other major cities on the west coast.*

3. *From the results of the raid on the Lucci Company, the FBI teams were pleased with their success. There were only two negatives: The head of the company, Larucci himself, was not on site. Neither was his son. Two folders were found with information and pictures naming Bill and*

Hammer. Retribution might not be over with, as long as the top people are on the loose. Therefore, I will contact the parties involved.

4. *The files the FBI had from the raid were probably the originals. With the new information obtained from the operation, there is hope that this raid and the confiscated information and arms will conclude any activity in the region. At this time it appears that al-Qaeda is now expunged from Alaska.*

Chapter 19

Spook knew that any coincidence for not finding the top leaders, as it was for the last operation, was very suspicious. Every operation, so far, had failed to turn up the masterminds or any information to their whereabouts. Both in Anchorage and now in Fairbanks, especially after the many hours of surveillance Spook and his partner had put in, the chances of the leaders not being where they were supposed to be was more than suspicious. These guys were slippery or there had to be a leak in someone's department.

The next day, Hammer received the bad news. The FBI agent had information, taken directly from the safe they had confiscated, that included files and pictures of Hammer and his family, the school the kids attended, and the house he lived in. In an additional file was information on Bill. Hammer was furious, but thanked the agent anyway. He asked the agent if he could have the files and it was agreed upon. That was the least he could do for all of the information he had been given by the two civilians. Hammer immediately called Spook and caught him just before he and Manny were leaving for the lower forty-eight. Hammer called Bill and arranged to meet at the motel as soon as possible.

The meeting between the four was not exactly cheery and carefree. The news from the FBI was shared. At this point, Hammer trusted Spook and knew that the two of them, he and Bill, now had a lot at stake. With the possibility of having any personal information in the hands of the terrorists and the top al-Qaeda cell members missing, their options were dwindling. Spook only had one suggestion and that was to totally disappear. Everything that could be traced had to go.

Hammer and Bill were not happy with the suggestion. Dumbfounded, they looked at each other and knew deep down that he was right. Hammer asked Spook where he could be contacted. He gave Hammer another card and they shook hands and left the motel.

Hammer and Bill talked the entire trip to the airport and on the way to Bill's lodge. They both knew the enormity of the task ahead. Bill's return to the lodge during the middle of his planned vacation, a disguise for helping with the raid on the Fairbanks buildings, and seeing his obvious withdrawn demeanor, was taken by the other workers as a sign of trouble. Bill just sat on the front porch of the lodge looking at Lake Iliamna, pondering the future. His main thought was, "My beautiful place is now gone." He could no longer be associated with the area at all if he was to disappear. After explaining the situation to his staff, Bill proposed an agreement with the cook and his wife and security man to become partners and to run the lodge themselves. They looked at each other and after a short conversation all agreed they would love to accept the offer. There was only one problem: they didn't have the money to buy the lodge.

Bill chuckled and said, "I was once in a position like you all are in and had help from a very special man, my dad. Here is the contract I had my lawyer in Anchorage draw up. I just received it on my e-mail." They all looked it over and then broke out in smiles, each signing on the dotted line. Bill made two copies and kept the original, which was to be recorded in Anchorage. He asked the group, "Are you three going to rename it or keep the current name?" The cook said that they should rename it for safety reasons and Bill agreed. He finished by saying, "All I need is the money and it will be yours." One of the three new owners handed Bill an old scuffed-up $1 bill. "I guess that's that," Bill said.

Hammer had stayed out of the whole process while waiting, knowing his turn would soon come in Dillingham. He loaded some of Bill's things and got the dogs in their traveling crates, returning to the steps in front of the lodge where he found Bill. Bill said to Hammer, "There go my dreams," and hung his shaking head. Hammer patted him on the back and said, "It's hard to lose what you've built up, but there are more dreams out there and I'm sure we'll all make it through this together." Hammer handed Bill a couple of Red Bulls and they both nodded and smiled at each other while getting up and heading for the airplane.

Just after landing at Dillingham, Bill made a call from the hangar to the *Anchorage Daily News*, stating that the lodge had been sold due to an illness of the previous owner who was not expected to live. He also put the signed contract in an envelope, addressed it and put it in the mailbox.

Hammer talked to Katie and made arrangements for her to assume ownership of the company, also signing over the business with forms from his lawyer. The house was to be sold by the bank and no ties would be left to any member of the family. The kids were told that they were going on a short vacation and withdrawn from school by Hammer without them knowing. Sandy checked in to the Department of Wildlife and arranged a leave of absence. All of the forwarding addresses were falsified. Hammer stored whatever they wanted in a container that would be eventually shipped to Anchorage and stored under the name Francis Pal. Hammer had removed some of the items from the original storage container, changed the name and paid for two years in advance. The remainder of the arms and confiscated material was left in a container and the number and location of that container were sent to the FBI agent.

Their two pups were put in traveling crates and along with the two of Bill's, prepared for trip. Hammer made arrangements with the local bank to open an account for Katie to help run the air service and left money for any needed supplies. The money from the house would also go into that account. No one was to know about any of the financial arrangements except a lawyer who had power of attorney for only that transaction for the house. Katie was extremely

147

emotional about them leaving, but understood the circumstances. Finally, all of Hammer's business transactions were called into the paper as Bill had done. The last thing that Hammer had asked Spook to do was make some false IDs for the two of them and miraculously he received them in the day's mail. He was amazed at the speed in which Spook worked, but didn't ask questions. There was no time.

Hammer had many friends in the airport, one of whom owned a reliable Cessna 421 Golden Eagle III and was willing to sell it. In the past, Hammer had done some work on the airplane and knew it was in good shape. Hammer had said, "Name your price," and his friend did, so Hammer paid cash for the plane. That afternoon, after all was said and done, the day after the last meeting with Spook, the two girls, three adults and four dogs climbed aboard the Golden Eagle III, which was loaded with fuel, food, a couple of duffle bags and a few changes of clothes. They taxied out for takeoff and took a last glance from the ground at Dillingham. There were no tears because the girls thought this was to be a vacation, not knowing they might not ever see the town again.

Hammer pushed the throttles forward, adding gradual full power, and the Golden Eagle III, with her two 375-horsepower-geared engines smoothly built up airspeed. The airplane cleared the ground and Hammer activated the gear motor, raising the landing gear, and he made a climbing turn to the north.

The Golden Eagle III was one of the faster reciprocating twins that Cessna made and with the load aboard, the aircraft showed no hesitation to gain altitude. Climbing from 5,000 feet to 8,500 feet, the path of the airplane would be to the north initially and then after ten miles and out of sight they made a turn to the opposite direction. They used this pattern as a ruse, reversing course when out of eye contact at every airport they landed at. Except Hammer and Bill, the others aboard were unsure of their route or destination and really didn't care at this time; the beauty of the valley floor and the mountains were breathtaking. Whatever location the plane was destined for, the family would be together and hopefully leave no trail.

Mark had been in Anchorage almost ten months now, way too long for him because his attitude had not improved. He had become more familiar with the rain and wind, but still longed for the sun to take the stiffness out of his joints, especially for serving. He played tennis indoors the entire winter, but there was no substitute for the outdoors and the hot sun.

His teams had been split up with half going to Denver and the other half divided elsewhere in the department. He had spent much of his time since the last raid analyzing the information found in the safe. There was a tremendous amount, revealing information that would surely help his position.

Names, companies, pictures, plans, shipping data and times, and even overseas destinations were all given. The cell had made a major mistake and the overconfidence of Larucci finally caught up with him. All was to Mark's satisfaction, except the fact that the man himself was like an eel, and had slipped away again. Two of the files he recovered were of extreme interest. The first file covered personnel profiles of the pilot and his family and the second contained information on the lodge owner. He had remembered the files specifically because when he had initially opened them, there were a few pictures of the civilians with large red Xs marked across them. He assumed they were on a hit list of some sort. Mark knew that Hammer and Bill had helped his team with information about the warehouse and larucci, yet he made no effort to contact them. Their information was invaluable and he thought to himself that a mistake would be made if he made no effort to notify them about the files. After all, if it wasn't for them, his teams would still be looking for the "elusive gunrunners".

There was a third file that was far more interesting. This eight-page file had named Saga Hans Rains, who had several aliases including "Dean Schroeder," as the informant and undercover man in the FBI. This information told of his background as a double agent and other hidden operatives in the FBI. All Mark saw when he found this file was a way out and a chance to finally clear his name.

Dean, his team member from St. Louis, had been on a two-week vacation in Seattle after he had taken part in the raid. The office called him back in, letting him know they had information about the cell and wanted to start another operation. Dean was back in no time and as he walked through the doors of the gray building, was arrested, shackled and flown to St. Louis.

With one mole in hand and the others pending, the gratitude of the agency who had been looking for the leak was made public. Mark felt better about himself as an agent, knowing that he had been exonerated from the fiasco in St. Louis. Dean had been tipping al-Qaeda to the times and places of the FBI raids. It was only fitting that Mark, himself, had captured Dean and produced the incriminating evidence that brought this agent to justice.

The majority of the documentation found in the small safe dealt with the larger cities on the west coast. Mark had immediately made reports and sent copies of the information to the head offices of these named cities, disclosing people, holdings, ships, and even aircraft belonging to and used by al-Qaeda. The different districts analyzed the information. The agency planned and executed a huge operation to take down the organization. The raids took place simultaneously in each city and were executed with perfection, becoming one of the most aggressive and successful operations of the FBI for gathering information and making arrests against al-Qaeda on American soil ever for the bureau.

Mark was now quite famous. The only thing that was missing was the top al-Qaeda member from his area, Larucci. Mark had no idea where he was. However, to Mark's approval, this highly anticipated day had come. He carried a file in his attaché, along with his laptop and blackberry, to the Denver office. Having been called in after things had calmed down, he was to meet with the deputy director at the Denver offices.

Marked entered the district chief's office looking dapper and suave and with great confidence. He was greeted by the chief himself with a handshake. Everyone wanted to meet Mark. He was escorted to a waiting area and was offered some refreshment. In five minutes a young attractive assistant escorted him to a boardroom and upon opening the door he was greeted by three men.

"Good morning Mark," the man at the head of the table said. "Please have a seat."

He introduced himself as deputy director and introduced the two others. He continued by stating, "Can you fill us in on your investigation?"

Mark replied with an affirmative and he began a forty-five minute overview showing documents and facts using computer and PowerPoint.

What was unusual was that during the presentation there was never a mention of civilian help. All of the information had been uncovered by his teams, including a large container of arms found at the airport. After he finished, the deputy director said that they were extremely impressed with the work and results of his Alaska unit. They were impressed that he was able to uncover such a large amount of information in the most difficult of situations. Also, uncovering any agency moles took some "serious effort." Not only were they grateful, but they offered him the position of deputy director to the Los Angeles district. Mark made an effort to look as if he was seriously thinking and then accepted.

A few days since the meeting and back in Anchorage, Mark had cleared his personal items from his office and packed them up to be sent down to LA. He said his last farewells to the chief and thanked him for his support. The remaining files of his teams' efforts were left in a bureau file room and marked, "CLOSED," except the very first one. It stated, "IN PROGRESS." The title of this folder was "Larucci, Toni" and when opened it was marked with the large black letters, "SUSPECT MISSING."

Part 3

Disappearing: A Means to a New Life

CHAPTER 20

The Golden Eagle flew north for about ten minutes until it was out of sight of Dillingham and any other of the smaller villages in the area. Hammer stayed low, descending near the mountain tops and sometimes below them, through the valleys and out of any possible radar coverage with his transponder off. He made a turn southeasterly at Aleknagik and hugged the hills, flying over Cook Inlet to Prince William Sound and past Cordova to Ketchikan for fuel. The Golden Eagle was fast, almost twice as fast as the Skymaster. They had taken the most direct route, gaining only the necessary altitude for winds and to conserve fuel. Hammer had chosen this particular airplane because it had extra auxiliary fuel tanks. The pressurization was an advantage too. If needed, they could fly above the clouds rather than through or below them, missing most of the more turbulent air.

All of the family was ready for a stop and they were relieved to stretch their legs and walk the dogs on the tarmac at Ketchikan. They stayed close to the airport and ate at the airport café. The girls wanted to go across the channel to the town, but Hammer did not want the possibility of being recognized. The hour and a half spent on the ground seemed a very short time and they were soon in the air again.

Departing to the north and shutting down the transponder after leaving the airport traffic area, they again circled out of sight to a heading of 184 degrees. Omak was the next planned stop. Hammer, knowing that he would have to file a flight plan to cross over the Canadian border, filed under a false number, the same aircraft number he and bill had changed on the outside of the plane before they had taken off from Dillingham. Hammer wanted no part of leaving a tail number to trace; al Qaeda had found him before. Fifty miles prior to crossing the border to Canada, Hammer called Vancouver Center and activated his flight plan. He gave them his altitude, heading, and destination, direct to Tacoma, a destination they would never make.

He and Bill were the only two who knew the final destination, and they had not shared the information with anyone. The weather was clear between two layers of clouds and with a healthy tailwind, the Golden Eagle whisked along at over 400 knots ground speed. As soon as they crossed the northern U.S. border, Hammer cancelled radar coverage, dropped down to 5,000 feet and flew direct to Omak. They flew east of Blain, with their flight path taking them north of Mount Baker. The rough-looking north cascades moved by rapidly and as soon as they could they descended to just above the tree tops.

Omak's airport was much smaller than Ketchikan's. The temperature was also much higher, a good thirty degrees Fahrenheit. A landing was made and the family was relieved to be on solid ground; at the least they were all glad not to have to sit any longer. The comfort of the airplane was nice, but games and conversation could only last so long; they were all getting grouchy and tired of traveling.

Hammer borrowed the airport car, an old '63 Chevy Biscayne station wagon usually left at the airport just for pilots and guests. The five of them piled in, leaving the dogs in the shade at the airport in their crates with water and food. They drove to a local restaurant in the small town and had a great meal of chicken-fried steak, mashed potatoes and gravy, corn on the cob and whole local farm milk; the main course was followed by a piece of homemade country-style apple pie. Since this was the heart of apple country, they had been tempted and finally persuaded to indulge in the decadent dessert, augmented with rich vanilla ice cream. Bloated to ecstasy with their meal, they all checked into one of the few motels. Bill and Sandy went back to the plane and picked up the dogs and luggage. Bill took time to change the N number on both sides of the airplane to another false ID. The family would rest in Omak, allowing Hammer and Bill a chance to plan and make arrangements for the next few days. Sandy and the girls toured the shops and took in a new movie.

During the entire time they were on the ground in Omak, Bill and Hammer were hoping the deception was working, using sporadic flying methods and keeping the transponder off. Flying activity was low and there was no indication that they were being followed. Years before, there would have been many aircraft using the same routes they had and the trail was sure to have been easily hidden, but in the existing state of aviation, with expensive fuel and other aviation costs, there was much less traffic; they hoped the plane would blend in to what little traffic there was. Sandy, Bill and Hammer were sure they had covered everything, but still took every precaution; all three carried .40 caliber Sig Sauer pistols.

The next leg of the trip was to Rock Springs, taking off from Omak, heading north and circling out of sight to any population. Turning back to a southeasterly heading, they flew toward Boise and on to Rock springs. All of the fuel and expenses were paid by cash, leaving no paper trail. If ever there was a question about the plane, it would be associated with a false tail number.

The Rock Springs airport was some distance from the city so the girls just stayed by the airport. Bill eased their desire to visit the small town by letting them know that they could shop and sightsee at the next stop. "This stop was planned just for fuel," he had said, knowing that the actual purpose was to stay away from larger airports and people. Movement created the possibility of being noticed.

The girls were not only getting ornery, but suspecting different motives than just vacationing. The dogs were walked and ran after every grasshopper and bug that moved in the prairie grass and tumbleweed beside the runway. Bill, in his reassuring voice, kept everyone calm until it was time to board the plane. He had anticipated this moment and planned to bring out a new game. The plan worked and as the 421 climbed and headed north and then toward the east side of the Rockies, the girls did not even notice the change of scenery. They were too engrossed in Cranium.

The next part of the plan was to drop down over the eastern rim of the Rockies, just above the valley floor and fly south past Fort Collins and the Boulder/Denver area, tucked in as close to the mountains as possible. Hammer would have his transponder off and fly slower to disguise the size of the airplane he knew was showing up as a blip on the radar. The destination of the family, still unknown to them, was Colorado Springs and Peterson Field. There, Hammer had made arrangements for an enclosed hangar, a hiding place for the plane, and a rented van for ground transportation.

The mountains to the west and the plains to the east made for a beautiful welcome. The outline of Pike's Peak stood above the rest of the mountains to the southwest and all eyes scanned the surrounding hills, absorbing the breathtaking beauty of the Rocky Mountains. Hammer finally told them they were almost at their final destination and he started concentrating on the landing. The girls had no clue for the geographic explanations and had never heard of theme parks in Colorado. Hammer called Peterson tower and was cleared for a straight in, as expected, and he began slowing the plane and extended the gear.

The ground felt so good that everyone became frisky and loud. They didn't care where they had landed and the girls took joy in helping unload the plane. The new hangar was large, enough room for two planes the size of the Golden Eagle and a small tug was waiting to push the plane in. Everyone helped transfer the bags to the van, except a couple of heavy duffle bags that were left in the plane. One of the newer hangars built on the field, the bifold doors were closed and latched with a remote control and they all piled in the van and headed for one of the nicer motels in the downtown Colorado Springs area, near the Antler Plaza. The dogs were given a good run in a local park on the way.

Checking in to the eight-story motel, they cleaned up and left their bags and the dogs in the room, making their way to the restaurant below. The restaurant was excellent and as they all ate and talked with a lot of laughter, Hammer realized that another day would be better for the news of their future plans. He wasn't ready to dish out the truth yet. Fatigue was almost instantaneous after the meal and they all were pleasantly lethargic from traveling and eating. They went to their rooms and slept.

The next day brought a more rested attentive group, with shopping and fun activities in store for the morning. The girls were wondering why the long stay in Colorado Springs and at lunch. Hammer finally quit the deception and explained the reasoning behind Colorado Springs. The atmosphere went from tired, but satisfied, to one of disbelief and a situation that brought both girls to tears. In some ways, both had suspicions as to the long, secretive trip. Hammer had to generate a positive environment with his new plans. Their trail, he was confident, had been swept clean and they would be safe in this part of the country. They would find a house in Woodland Park, a small community west of Colorado Springs, to give them an appearance of being military or working at the fort. The beautiful scenery had worked once and, although not as picturesque as the ocean and wildlife surrounding Dillingham, Pike's Peak and the Rockies offered varieties of trees, water, and magnificent color, creating their own magnetism.

The small community of Woodland Park was continually growing and was composed of civilians and military personnel who supported Fort Carson, as well as merchants in town. Some even worked at or attended the Air Force Academy, located just north of Colorado Springs. Pretending to be military would hide the family's real identity, or at least they could blend in with neighbors who actually worked at the fort. Hammer and Bill made all of the arrangements. Everything had to be purchased. They had plenty of money in accounts that could not be traced. However, their new identification had to be treated with discretion; they didn't want anyone to be suspicious of their past history or where they were from.

Sandy and the girls found a house they had to have. The two-story farm-style structure was in a new development and Hammer spent little time purchasing it. It was not too elegant and would not draw attention, but they each had their own rooms and there was a large backyard with a swimming pool and a separate garage. Hammer and Bill spent time adding the necessary accoutrements: a gun safe, alarms, lights, cameras, and whatever else they could think of to keep them safe. One could say they were fanatical, but having dealt firsthand with al-Qaeda, they took no chances. The girls became acquainted with their new school and being near the size of Dillingham's, they fit right in. Most of the kids in this school had families that moved around frequently, so the addition of a few more was not unusual.

Hammer grew a mustache and Bill lost a little weight. He also started wearing better clothes and a pair of sunglasses, which the girls teased him continuously as being one of the "Blues Brothers." He enjoyed the attention. Hammer arranged for the 421 to be refurbished with new engines, a new glass panel and a new interior and exterior, all provided by a company in Texas. He and the rest of the family flew down and dropped the plane off at the Fort Worth airport, catching another plane to Orlando at the last moment. Disney World would help cheer up the whole family. Hammer felt he had to keep their spirits up in hopes of forgetting the past year's events.

How long they stayed in Woodland Park would depend on their ability to remain hidden. Hammer made every possible attempt to make the transition interesting. Trips to Denver and the zoo along with shopping and great restaurants were activities in the large city that were interesting to the girls. To the west, the Rocky Mountains presented great hiking and good old high-lake fishing. Ghost town exploration was a big hit and kept them all occupied for several weekends. Hammer hoped the girls would find Colorado as interesting as he remembered it to be when he was young. He didn't know how long they would be in Woodland Park or if they would ever leave.

As the family became acclimated to the higher altitude, they all enjoyed the outdoor life and what the Rockies had to offer. January had come and the Christmas holiday had been spent in Florida. Even with all of the fun and excitement, there was still no place like home;

they were all glad to be back. School and new friends were what the girls liked most and it was back to business for everyone else.

Hammer set up several large computers in his den. He was still obsessed with finding al-Qaeda and confident enough to feel that he had the ability to get information about the cell if it was out there. He also learned new skills and how to get ongoing cases and past files from different agencies. His experience would help track the cell and with his self confidence in high gear, finding Larucci and his terrorists as they moved around the States would now be his full-time obsession. He was intent on ridding his family of the burden of hiding. All he needed was time and a chance to work his methods. The task would not affect his first responsibility, his family, but he was confident that he had the ability to both protect and investigate.

Hammer was driven and spent countless hours a day cross-referencing and looking for clues to the phantom unit, pounding keys to reveal the unknown and discovering clues to the whereabouts of Larucci. It was mesmerizing, looking in the computer screen for Larucci as Hammer knew he had to find the cell before it found him. He would win the race this time.

After awhile, spending so much time obsessed, he would forget about the passage of time and he found himself awake and dreary-eyed in the early morning, having worked the entire night. He hoped the girls understood and always made the excuse that his efforts were necessary for their safety, which in actuality was not the entire truth. He also wanted vengeance!

Jackie and Amanda fit right in to the new school nestled in a beautiful setting in Woodland Park. The neighbors were friendly and there were many children his kids' ages. Bill was happy with the satellite system and the sixty-inch plasma screen in the family room. He was also appreciative of the small refrigerator next to the couch for refreshments. Hammer knew Bill had to have some old conveniences. Sandy took to task and made the house livable. She set up a training gym in the basement and made use of the large outside pool in the backyard for laps. The girls and the dogs all loved the large backyard to play in.

Besides the cell, the only thing worrying Hammer was Bill's health. He was noticeably slower at certain things. His hand movements, walking and just even daily movements were slowing down. Hammer had to lure him into seeing a doctor; he knew Bill wouldn't seek medical care on his own. Bill forced Hammer to be cunning, a process he was good at with two teenagers, but the necessity was especially important for Bill's health problems. Hammer had assumed Bill had taken care of any medication in Anchorage. If Hammer met with resistance, so be it. The solution would probably end with handcuffs and being dragged to a clinic.

Hammer had been corresponding with the rebuilders of the airplane and was given a date to pick up the Golden Eagle. The refurbishment had taken longer than anticipated, due to a few corrosion areas and having to remove and replace a panel or two. The Alaskan climate is definitely hard on aircraft and some of that salty air caused pinholes in a few lower panels. He and Bill caught a flight out of Peterson Field to Dallas/Fort Worth, picked up a rental car, and traveled to a small strip where the aircraft company was located.

The plane turned out beautifully, with a bright white base coat overall and trimmed in burgundy and dark blue designs on the sides and tail, outlined with silver. Hammer didn't want it to cause too much attention. The new gold-heated window with new boots for ice and the new comet strobes on the tip tanks put the finishing touches on the exterior. The interior was buckskin leather with a darker navy blue carpet. The interior panels were a soft white. The avionics, engines and props were all new. In fact, almost everything was new. Hammer realized that with new avionics, he was glad to have had some down time with the manuals and the disks for computer interactive study. The Garmin GPS system was much more sophisticated than any of the previous systems he had used.

The flight from Texas to Colorado was brief and when he and Bill got closer to Peterson Field, Hammer put in a call to Sandy to pick up the girls and meet at the hangar. Their new hangar on the southeast side of the field was immaculate. He had covered the floor with two coats of epoxy in a light gray that was like a mirror. He also had a complete mechanic's tool bench and a roll-away in red and black for his tools near a work bench in one of the corners. The other corner was divided into rooms, one for lounging and watching television and a separate room for Hammer's computer on an oak desk with a matching chair. There was a hidden panel next to the bathroom that opened to a large gun safe. The items he and Bill had brought back from Dillingham were kept inside. The whole building was air conditioned.

Most of the work had been done by Hammer and James, a new friend, a fellow pilot who he had met at the airport. James, a few years younger than Hammer, had been interested in the plane when it first landed and had seen them unloading. Not needing to be asked, he was always there to help push or wash the airplane. James also volunteered to help with anything, just to be near the planes.

James' main interest was helping the air explorers on the field, a group of high school kids who had an interest in aviation. He volunteered his time for fundraisers and other events to help educate and introduce the younger, less privileged kids and to help them earn money for flying. On occasion, James would save enough of his veteran's money to take some of the kids flying in a 150. It was not much, but the flights meant everything to the kids. James fit right in with the family and on many occasions went on trips with them. He lived on the outskirts of town in a rundown shack with his daughter, a student at the local junior college.

Sandy and the girls watched as the sparkling Golden Eagle made its approach and landed, taxiing to the hangar. At first sight they all loved the plane with all of its new paint and gloss and agreed on the nickname Lucky Lucy after the *Peanuts* character. James suggested a person on the field paint the name on the fuselage. The girls were overjoyed so Hammer agreed. The new tail numbers, finally legalized, had also been changed. One of the joys of the whole family was to spend a morning at the hangar and help Hammer or James wash, clean and wax her. Of course that didn't last long, being so much work.

The days in Woodland Park moved by quickly. While the girls were at school, Hammer would search the web and place calls, hoping for a lead. Whatever popped into his view or came to mind to find Larucci was important. Wherever a trail led him, he would follow. He carried a small notebook for recording any new thoughts he had while working at the hangar or on the plane; he wrote down thoughts to be pursued at a later time or he just moved to the computer at the hangar. On occasion, Hammer would go from home to hangar or to any place where he could concentrate the most. Bill would be just the opposite; he mostly just watched old John Wayne movies, his favorite.

Hammer had read most of the available FBI accounts involving Alaska and any terrorist activity the bureau had published. There was not much available, but the reports cited the bureau with "splendid work, featuring raid after raid, confiscating buildings, ships and aircraft." Prisoners were questioned and sources were revealed, leading to operations in San Francisco and Seattle that put a stop to the al-Qaeda attempts of terrorism in the continental United States and Alaska. Several agents were credited for obtaining information and were awarded various honors and credits and on and on. One thing Hammer noticed was that he and Bill were never mentioned. Neither was the most important fact, that moles were found in the FBI.

One Tuesday, Hammer had just finished mowing his large back lawn and dumping the cut grass in the compost pile near the back fence. He parked the small John Deere mower in the shed and headed for the computer room, grabbing a cold Red Bull from the refrigerator on the way. His thoughts were on the usual: Larucci's trail from Fairbanks. He remembered that the last report stated, "The FBI claimed credit for eliminating the threat of a terrorist cell in both Seattle and San Francisco. They had coordinated the raids and confiscated equipment, arresting men in both cities. The special terrorist units had found some information during the raids and, along with fact finding through interrogation of prisoners, subpoenas were issued to support action against other known al-Qaeda cells."

Where could Larucci have gone? He had to have a larger city to hide in and a place for shipping and receiving. The feds had stopped looking for the cell, convinced they had succeeded in its elimination. Hammer kept patiently looking for what he was missing in cities up and down the coast. He was sure that the cell would relocate—its terrorists were too confident to disappear. Finally, the proverbial light bulb in his head went on and with a pure guess his thoughts led him to what he was looking for. After months of coming up empty-handed, having great ideas and being constantly lead to dead ends, good fortune struck again in the form of pictures. Evidently Larucci was still so confident, so daring and so cocky, he didn't care if his picture was plastered on the local newspaper. A picture of Tony Larucci appeared on the screen in front of him, originating from Portland, of all places. The city was so close to past cells that Hammer hadn't fully looked into the possibilities. This was the lead he had been patiently waiting for all this time.

Hammer searched for facts and company names. He thought it would be easy now, with pictures of the board of directors and specifics in the form of addresses and telephone numbers. He needed to find all the facts. He inquired to the secretary of state for corporation information and found none. He went to the Crown Corporation, the old conglomerate Larucci had used, and found nothing.

Finally he went to the "sounds like" function and plugged them in. Immediately a site appeared with a small article from a daily paper mentioning the Larrue Company in Portland, from several months ago. Bingo! This is what he was looking for! He and Bill had come all this way to get away from the terrorists and they were only a short thousand miles away. He didn't know if that was far enough. The puzzle was finally taking shape. Hammer's luck was changing and he could feel the positive vibes of success. He would keep looking and get more information. There would have to be no doubts. With that little positive moment in his mind, and thinking of more directions to follow, his eyes tired from another day of focusing on the screen; his eyes slowly closed, no longer able to keep sleep away.

Waking in his leather chair the next morning, a usual event in the past months, Hammer had had enough of the computer and just wanted to work on the plane and clean it up; some good old fashion knuckle-busting busy work to let him think. The flight back from Texas had added about ten pounds of weight to the plane, all from bugs. He hadn't realized it had been over a week since the trip and he drove down to the hangar and pressed the remote control that opened the door. There was a small creaking in one of the hinges as the door opened, so he grabbed his ten-foot ladder, climbed to the top and applied a small amount of LPS 2. Applying a little of the dark-colored liquid on the hinge pins and mechanisms should do the trick as he recycled the bifolding contraption. The irritating sound was gone. He climbed back down, folded the ladder and put it back in its storage position.

He hooked up the vacuum and was about to clean the pilot and copilot area of the airplane when he realized it was spotless. He grabbed a handful of rags and was about to wipe down the glare shield, but it too was spotless. He backed up to survey the whole front of the plane and upon inspection, there was not one bug, spot of dirt, or dried water droplet. By that time, James was standing next to him, admiring the beautiful airplane. Hammer mentioned to James that he had been busy. James retorted with, "She looks nice, doesn't she?" And then he added, "Ah, looks like I missed something!" Grabbing a towel, he headed for a missed spot under the right flap. One of the main tires looked a little low and Hammer didn't have a nitrogen tank so James quickly ran off and in minutes came back with a small tank on wheels. He added a few pounds to each tire to equalize the pressure.

James had a hard life, but one wouldn't know from his attitude. His demeanor was always friendly and he had a genuine smile. Coming from an area in the south were the small towns had a hometown magnetism that kept generation after generation from leaving and marriages at an extremely early age, his ambition was not on the farms. Physical-labor jobs were a dime a dozen. He saw through the temptations of staying in the same town for a lifetime, not ever having experienced the outside, and left at the age of seventeen. Enlisting in the army for no other reason than a lack of money to support school, James became a mechanic, going to aircraft school and taking honors in his class. His only problems were his seemingly slow mannerisms but this definitely wasn't true.

James wanted to be a pilot but was sent to Vietnam as one of the many needed mechanics for helicopters, staying for just one tour. He was then sent back to Bragg and finally given a chance to attend flight school. Not much was available except helicopters so with the advice of his commanding officer he signed up to become a warrant officer and attend flight school. He was granted acceptance to the program, again making the top of his class, showing his new bars on his epaulets and being the top pilot of his flight wing. Having combat experience already, he was sent to Vietnam soon after graduation; having in-country experience as a mechanic and never seeing actual combat made no difference. He had a successful first six months. His tenacity and willingness to help his fellow soldiers earned him the nickname Gator since he was from the south. That thick southern accent was identifiable by most in the region and he soon became a comfort to those on the ground in need. His radio conversations were identifiable by both friendly and enemy ears, creating a space at the top of the list of the most wanted list by the Vietcong.

Not only was he successful, but lucky, having been shot down twice. The first time he was forced to land from ground fire in a remote clearing, not knowing if he was going to live or die. On the ground and just after the impact in enemy territory, he checked himself over and couldn't find any holes, just a few minor cuts and scratches and a couple of dislocated fingers. He then pulled his copilot from the burning fuselage and kept him and his door gunner under cover. Aided by his side arm and the M-60 taken from the door gunner position, he kept the surrounding North Vietnamese at bay until a rescue could be made. In between the bursts of machinegun rounds, his hands felt like they were on fire. He taped his fingers together so he could at least support and load the weapons, which eased the pain a little.

His second forced landing was again from ground fire. Smoke filled the cockpit and he was forced to set the craft down deep behind unfriendly lines. The mission was for an extraction of seriously wounded soldiers. His crew was okay, but the helicopter looked finished. The men were starting to panic so he established a crude skirmish line. With more freedom to move about, he surveyed the helicopter and with some ingenuity and expertise as a mechanic, somehow astonishingly got the machine back off the ground and nursed it to the LZ where he picked up three wounded and made it back to the base hospital. The unit CO was so flabbergasted after seeing the condition of the machine that he submitted James for a decoration.

After several weeks of R&R, James was back in the driver's seat, delivering ammo and troops to the camps as before. In the eleventh month of that year, shortly before the end of the conflict, James suffered from the effects of battle fatigue. He had done and seen enough, working harder in one year than most had in two. The final straw was seeing a line of young men in bags inside one of the hangars going home. James walked into the medical tent with jungle fever, a rash over half his body, suffering from malnutrition, and with nerves that were shot. He spent a year recuperating in a military hospital in Germany and was discharged a month after he was stateside, never seeing or receiving any gratitude for his years of combat.

Going from job to job as Bill had done, James was always looking for something. It had taken fifteen years for him to realize that the Vietnam conflict was over and to move on. The catalyst was flying. He still loved to fly and the goal of a private fixed-wing certificate snapped him out of the funk he carried in his mind from being brutalized by the war. He didn't want to fly professionally, just for fun, and saved all of his extra money for the air time. He worked at the local car dealership as a mechanic and specialized in diagnostics. The local mechanics who worked with him knew that his slow methods were much faster in many cases than the computer. They all liked him and came to him when they needed help. The military was not going to help him. They had forgotten him.

CHAPTER 21

Bits and pieces of information turned into leads and sources, pathways to what Hammer was after. He meticulously compiled and organized two large file boxes of material containing articles, pictures and facts that would help make Portland the likely hideout. Lucci, Larrue or Larucci, whatever the name, seemed to be the key and he found what he was looking for in Portland's archives of daily newspapers online. Pictures and reports, including stories concerning prominent businessmen with sons in their twenties as partners or co-owners listed as one of the three names, were occasionally mentioned. The cell still seemed to have no remorse for their activities or fear of being exposed. He backtracked, not wanting to miss anything, searching Los Angeles, San Francisco and Seattle again and again for the slightest clues to tie names to known criminals in Portland. Without actually being in the cities, it was difficult to follow or recognize the Larucci family. He only had older newspaper-quality pictures.

Bill was some help, but not much. Hammer would call him in for a positive ID when new pictures were found. If there was ever a need to leave the safety of Colorado Springs in search of Larucci, there would have to be no doubts to his location and identity; a hundred percent accuracy to the location would be needed. By now, Hammer was convinced that the girls could not take another move. Being spotted, even in town, was a risk he was not willing to take.

Little did Hammer know that the discovery of his family was the least of Tony Larucci's concerns.

Tony was devastated and was not used to taking second chair. Not only did he lose both of his companies, one in Anchorage and the other in Fairbanks, but all of the precious arms and explosives stored in his hiding places were gone. He also lost two training camps and two of his most coveted friends and comrades in Darby and Chuck. They did most of his work and were invaluable. He would never be able to replace them. His ships, aircraft and warehouses in Alaska were all gone. This was an enormous emotional loss and, needless to say, very expensive. Tony thought he would outsmart the authorities in Anchorage by relocating all of the crates of arms and explosives to the hidden basements of the warehouses before the FBI moved in. He was sure everything was safe, but his men, observing from nearby, said that the FBI had left without finding the stash. There was no clue to the identity of the other people who followed, finding the arms. Sooner or later he would know who they were and get even.

He had not expected the raid in Fairbanks and if it weren't for his secret room, he knew he would now be a guest of the US government. His snitch had no time to alert him to the unexpected raid and the result was a total surprise. The guard at the front desk had sounded the silent alarm to the upper floor and Tony had used his secret room for cover. After the FBI left, he, along with a small amount of money and a few documents taken from his desk, escaped down an entrance in the basement, heading for the larger of his two undiscovered warehouses. He was sure they would be secure. However, when he arrived, the telltale yellow ribbon of the authorities, marked as FBI, and the blockades on the streets surrounding the buildings were in place. A large eighteen-wheeler was being loaded from the basement; the building was already half-empty. This infuriated Tony to no end. He had seen enough and to get him out of his frustrated tone, he flagged down a cab and picked up one of his favorite ladies, proceeding to his secret apartment to drink himself into a stupor while lounging in the hot tub.

As soon as Tony could he called his son in Portland and told him to lay low. "Stop large shipments," he advised his son. Tony knew that the authorities had his small safe from the office and the contents he was unable to take with him would compromise the whole west coast network. When pieced together and translated, the entire operation could be destroyed. The money wasn't important, but the information could ruin the scheme they were planning. He assumed it to be too late for Seattle and San Francisco, but he could save Portland. Maybe if he hadn't waited so long in the little room he could have saved the others.

From Fairbanks, Tony carefully made his way to Ketchikan by small plane and then flew a short hop to Washington. He rented a car out of Bellingham, to be less conspicuous, and drove to Portland. Tony was glad to see his son, Eli, the face of a man he could depend on and feel at ease with. It was Eli who had the foresight to build the secret room in the office in Fairbanks. Portland was ripe for their operations and Tony and his son would take full advantage of any and all of what they could. As the greetings relaxed, Eli gave Tony the news that, as in Anchorage and Fairbanks, Seattle and San Francisco had all been compromised. All of their assets, except in Portland, had been seized by the government.

The FBI had taken little time to take possession of al-Qaeda's southern properties and, upon hearing the news, Tony had again been downright demoralized. It was hard to believe that Tony could maintain focus and find good in something now. Tony's thoughts were mostly with the FBI's ability to carry out two sequentially timed raids on the hidden cell's inventory of weapons in such a short time. He consoled himself without sorrow and was sparked by being an adversary of the mighty United States, probably quite high on the infidels' list of most wanted criminals. Whether FBI, CIA, NSA, or any other of the alphabet soup agencies, he knew he was much more intelligent than them. He smirked while blowing a ring of smoke from his Cuban cigar. After all, he was still a free man. The authorities could not and would not catch him. He was too smart for any of them, speaking of the infidels, and on their own turf. Being more pessimistic, he thought about how the authorities had destroyed his years of work; realizing his pet projects were all but lost. He was on his own now, not daring to contact his fellow al-Qaeda. His deep hiding would continue and only a few remaining tasks would draw him out. One of the tasks was to help his son succeed in his business. Another was to raise as much havoc as possible with the infidels with what resources he had. The loss was immense, with Portland his one and only last hope. He would find out the name of the agent in charge and somehow deal with him, his only bright thought at the moment. A smile soon came to his lips as he thought about another bright spot, his son and how they would triumph and defeat these worthless humans together.

Eli was satisfied with running the smaller Portland company. He was satisfied with the area and had a nice house and a great little bungalow near Tillamook, overlooking the Pacific Ocean. Eli had taken Portland by surprise, concealing the takeover of a small company and its holdings of a warehouse and a separate office building in his name. He needed a place to store shipments coming in from his dad. Now he was the only source for terrorist supplies on the west coast. He would transport containers from Portland with his own trucks either to Seattle or Eugene for shipment by ocean-going ship or rail. Nothing from Eli's company left by ship in Portland, the containers would be in jeopardy of being found in his own town, bringing suspicion to his location. Shipments coming in would either come through Tacoma or Eugene. They didn't have to be placed in warehouses; the trailers could just be parked and left anyplace for a short time. "Less local movement meant less visibility," Eli's motto indicated that he was smart like his dad, but controlled every aspect of the transportation and left nothing in the hands of others.

At the rate he was going, his operation would soon be larger than anything his father had done. Nonetheless, his company was not less effective or made less money; he was not competing, just providing the necessary equipment to his fellow terrorists. His company was less visible and Eli meant to keep it that way.

With a dark complexion and a slender but well-toned build, Eli was good-looking, hiding the fact that his easy-going attitude cloaked his vicious demeanor, even more so than his father's. He was the one who led the takeover of Bill's lodge and Hammer's house, doing the shooting of the cook and the dogs. The only reason he shot the cook was because the cook wouldn't make one of his favorite foods. He also killed the one at Dillingham, the pilot's dog, and would have succeeded with burning the place down if they hadn't tripped the alarm. He subconsciously summed up the situation by thinking "Why do these infidels have these filthy creatures in their houses?"

His tolerance was growing thin. He wanted to kill more frequently. He always carried a silenced model 92 Berretta. He used that gun because he liked the feel and it produced the impact that stimulated him to the highest. The sound of an infidel's death was his joy, exciting him to the maximum by robbing the existence of one's pitiful human life. If a dirty job came along, he was the first to volunteer and would feel hurt if he wasn't given the task. He would shoot anyone anytime; he didn't care. The infidels were easy targets and he enjoyed hearing them beg for their useless lives. Now, being on the top rung, he had *carte blanche* and could do anything he pleased.

Eli's weakness was women. He used and abused them and then dumped them. Eli had no trouble finding young ladies his age with his money, good looks and toys. After all, he spent much of his money on making himself look good. Eli was the male version of a female black widow spider combined with the brutality of a female grizzly protecting her cubs. He would find his prey at the more expensive clubs, wining and dining them and giving them a helicopter ride to his bungalow. The bungalow was located south of Tillamook on the ocean highway and was secluded. The nearest neighbors were miles away.

He would entertain them in his way and then seek special favors. The girls that were willing were given a ride back to Portland. Those that weren't willing were smacked around, wrapped in burlap sacks and weighted down, then given a ride fifteen miles out to sea. They were dropped from an altitude of 2,000 feet into the depths of the ocean. Again, he didn't care. The girls that made it back to Portland had no idea how close they had come to disaster. Eli just figured there were plenty of girls to be had.

Toni, on the other hand, had his list of desirable local women. He was more into experience and the old ways. His ladies were older and ladies who were good company. The difference between Toni and Eli was that Toni treated his women well and received the benefits.

Toni realized it would be difficult for him to be traced to Portland. His only flaw in Fairbanks was not leaving a charred body in the building, ending any possible search for him. He assumed his trail was cold. No one knew where he was except his son and a few cell members overseas. Toni knew his son was tightlipped and smart.

Hammer was tired and unable to find any more information on the Larrue Company. The trail had vanished for the time being. He was getting frustrated from his time spent in front of the computer. Trying to keep a positive outlook was difficult. Still, like a bird dog on point, he kept in the hunt. The paper trail seemed to just come to a stop. Finally, the day had come when he was at an impasse with his system. Fatigue had set in, the product of too much time being obsessed and not enough rest or variation of subject. He dragged Bill from the television room for a talk. The two discussed their options while sitting on the front porch in the sun, overlooking Pike's Peak to the southeast. Hammer needed a change and to be away from any mention of al-Qaeda. Obsession was a hard thing to overcome and fatigue was now in his eyes and mind as well.

Hammer didn't know if Bill had kept his appointment or not; Bill had not mentioned it either way. All he knew was that Bill's health was deteriorating and his condition was getting obviously worse day by day. His absentmindedness and lethargic mannerisms were becoming more obvious; he did not want to do anything. His reaction time was poor and his everyday facial expressions and head movements were freaking out the girls. Bill's reasoning was, "Who wasn't feeling this way as he grew older?"

Sandy and Hammer talked. She was concerned about the girls and the family in general. They had everything and maybe that was the problem. They were leading essentially an existence as a "family of things." Responsibility for chores had gone down the tube. Anything they wanted, they got. This was not like the simple way of life they had known in Alaska. Up there, they had everything they needed in life with just the simple things. Here, in Woodland Park, the family was not first--objects and things were. The girls had replaced family with other interests. Could it be their age? Hammer didn't know.

Hammer admitted he wanted everything for the girls, a reward for the hardship since Suzanne had died. Sandy wanted to get back to the old ways when the chance came. "They had everything with just being a family in Alaska," Sandy said. As it was now, the family was being torn apart.

Hammer needed the proverbial slap in the face, having been beaten down by constant rejection and the inability to find what he was seeking. Everyone needs an adjustment sometimes and Hammer was no different. The boost that Sandy had given him was the wakeup call he needed to snap him out of his daydream from fatigue. He was feeling more rejuvenated, more of his old self, and ready to continue his eagerness, assuring everyone that the end of their problems was near. He knew Portland was the place and any answers would be found there. By reason of deduction and the facts he had found, every trail had pointed him to Portland and it was the logical place to look for his nemesis. The pattern of movement seemed right and the smaller city was a natural lair for the corrupt cell. Portland was where he and Bill had decided to send a team.

The two planned a flight to a location to cover their hiding place. They were so paranoid about being found by anyone that they even decided not to use the local phones that could be traced. They climbed aboard Lucky Lucy and headed for Laramie, a place to initiate a call to Spook" by landline. That way, Spook" would know where they were. Hammer took off to the south and within ten miles turned 180 degrees, hugging the bases of the mountains west of the Springs to Fort Collins. Just past the antennas of Fort Collins they dropped down to an even lower altitude and flew directly to Laramie and landed.

At the airport, Hammer retrieved a card from his wallet and dialed the number on the touch-tone phone in the pilot lounge. On the third ring, Spook answered. Hammer replied, "Bill and I would like to hire you and Manny again." The conversation was short and to the point, with Spook agreeing. They settled on Salt Lake City for a meeting place in two days.

Hammer, with his boxes of organized material for Spook, felt he had enough information for a team to get started with an onsite investigation. Stowing the boxes and a full duffle bag in the cargo compartment located behind the last row of seats in Lucky Lucy, Bill made sure everything was secure while Hammer checked out the airplane. Hammer did a quick fuel drain and noticed a slight bulge in a tire. He thought that he was always adding nitrogen to the tires. Easily irritable with having to attend to the slightest tasks of a preflight checklist, he took the cover off of the pitot tube and moved to the nose for a quick glance at the Janitor cabin heater. He closed the baggage compartment in the snout and climbed up the air stair, pulling the door closed behind him.

Hammer walked to his seat through the center isle of the main cabin and sat to the left in the pilot's seat. He loved flying the 421, even grouchy as he was, and could never get enough. His mood, the product of wanting to act on the cell now, would change the minute they were airborne. Real fliers were like that. They could have all the problems in the world, but once they were in an airplane or in the air, it was like a pacifier. Bill was already in the right seat and strapped in; his hat partially covered his eyes in a snooze position.

Going through the checklist, Hammer verified circuit breakers and flipped the masters; he checked the voltage level of the battery. The rotating beacon was next, followed by a quick glance around the plane. He scanned the gauges that came to life on the panel and he pushed the prop and mixture levers full forward. Continuing, he moved the bank of mag switches to the on position and smoothly exercised the throttle levers for full motion, leaving them about a half-inch open. A touch of prime was all Lucky Lucy ever needed and he activated the left engine start switch. After two rotations the engine came to life with a rumble and a slight puff of smoke. Again Hammer checked readings and then went through the same procedure for the right engine. He verified quantities, pressures and vacuum; all checked okay. He depressed the avionics switch so he could communicate with Bill without having to yell. Continuing down the checklist he announced "Seatbelts," and then "Flaps," "Controls," and "Instruments." Each item checked okay so he was ready for flight in the complex aircraft.

He pushed the throttles forward another half inch, bringing the engines to a moderate rumble at 1,500 RPMs. Both engines were given time to warm the oil. From the inside of the fuselage, the sound of the engines was pleasantly baritone, while on the outside they were creating a definite sound of a throaty, aggressive attitude.

Hammer radioed ground control and received approval to taxi to the active runway, repeating the instructions. He went through what was left of his preflight checklist on the move, that old habit, and at the run-up area finished his mag checks and cycled the props, lowering the flaps to ten degrees with a movement of the switch to two detents.

Hammer made a final check of his flight instruments and glanced at the oil pressure. Taxiing to the hold line and stopping, he called the temporary tower for takeoff approval and was cleared for intersection B-6 on runway 30, followed by a crosswind departure. He added a little power and taxied to the centerline, turning to face 300 degrees. Verifying his directional gyro for heading, he then continued adding power. When Lucky Lucy was given the juice she set him back in the seat. She flew straight out at 300 degrees, lifting off at eighty knots and climbing out at 110. At 500 feet, she turned to the crosswind. Hammer headed directly for Salt Lake City, noting the distance of this flight would be far enough to keep them from exposing their hiding place.

The load aboard was light with full fuel and just the two of them, so the aircraft performance was outstanding. Hammer verified the name, entered the station identifier for the intended destination in the Garmin 480 GPS, and adjusted for the desired altitude. He finished by pressing a small button on the yoke, activating the auto pilot. The weather was VFR and the winds were good below 18,000 so he wouldn't talk to anyone until the approach at Salt Lake. Hammer had decided to get a little rest and give himself a chance to think about the meeting. Bill could monitor the instruments if he stayed awake. Hammer still kept one eye open as he sipped a Red Bull.

In a little over two hours, the winds growing a little stiff out of the northwest the closer they got to the west coast, Bill and he landed at the Salt Lake City Municipal Airport. The airport was a good size for their purpose and they didn't have to deal with too many of the bigger commercial jets. Bill had been listening to the CD player connected to the audio panel and napping the whole trip. Hammer noticed Bill was sleeping more and his facial muscles were making unusual movements when he was asleep. Hammer made another mental note to set up yet another appointment for Bill when they got back. He knew he would have to hogtie the lug to get him to go.

They taxied to the transient parking area and called for the fuel truck. Hammer watched the process as Bill went for the rental car. They loaded the duffle bag and plastic boxes in the car and headed for downtown Salt Lake and the Hilton on Temple. They met Spook on the sixteenth floor in an elegant suite, shaking hands and exchanging pleasantries over a couple of sparkling waters. Hammer always wanted to be ready for flying so he never had hard drinks, another old habit.

He explained the material he had and the process he had used to obtain what was there. Spook was glad to have the files and it gave him at least a starting point. Hammer also handed him a satellite phone for communications. They couldn't keep flying to Laramie every time he needed to talk to Spook. Spook explained how he would proceed and Hammer asked if there was anything else they could do or they needed. Hammer replied, "Negative." Since there was no more information to be shared, Hammer motioned to Bill and they headed for Spencer's, a local restaurant noted for its large steaks and baked potatoes.

They both had their fill and then headed for the airport, mostly ready for a nap. Hammer wanted to be back for an evening with the girls so they loaded a few things aboard and were soon airborne, heading due east for fifty miles and then taking a route directly to Grand Junction, Alamosa and then around the mountains to Colorado Springs. His thinking was that if one could follow him on this route to their home, they were good, but no one could. Speed and low level flight was hard to follow. Hammer believed in the old psychology that if one wants to stay hidden, never do anything the same way more than once. These thoughts were good and all, but what about the facilities and capabilities of the higher authorities? This was something that Hammer never did think of. He did remember what Spook had said earlier: "As long as there's a Larucci on the loose, deception will be the plan of action, no matter how tedious." Hammer told Bill to wake him if there was a need and then he shut his eyes.

They arrived back in Colorado Springs in about the same amount of time as the flight to Salt Lake. Favorable winds helped considerably and after the landing and as soon as the props stopped, there was James, standing ready to help push the plane in to the hangar.

Walking around the nose and forward wing areas, they looked at the amount of bugs they had imported from Salt Lake. James stated that if they were to leave the plane out, he would wash and put it away for him. Hammer was overjoyed at the offer and he and Bill headed home. James loved that airplane and he wanted to keep it looking shiny with a good scrub job. Lucky Lucy was certainly lucky to be washed so much by James. He was not only meticulous, but he always waxed the heavy bug areas.

Two weeks had passed since Hammer and Bill had spoken to Spook and they both were thinking that Spook might be in over his head or suffering from a cold trail finding Larucci.

On Saturday the satellite phone rang. No surprise, it was Spook. He wanted to meet and share information. He and his partner were in Portland and would meet Hammer and Bill at the Courtyard in Hillsborough the next day. Hillsborough was a small community to the west of Portland.

Hammer went to his charts and calculated the time and route. If they were lucky they might make it in a little over five hours with a stop. He planned for six, with low pressure sending in a strong southwesterly wind. They left early the next day and stopped at Ontario, Idaho for fuel and a well-needed stretch. Continuing on to Hillsborough, they landed, picked up a car, and made it to the motel just in time for the noon meeting.

At first, the meeting produced good news and was informative. Spook told Hammer and Bill that he and Manny had spent most of the time on stakeouts and had gathered plenty of material. The bad news was it wasn't enough for a justified operation. Bill verified pictures of Larucci. After opinions, all four accepted the recommendations of Spook and agreed that more information was needed. *"Absolutely sure"* were the two key words. Spook was not going to speculate on the time it might take to complete the task, but seemed to think they were close. They would not settle for anything less than the capture of everybody this time. They had to know every move and how each person was involved. Two more people were needed for the operation and that would be Hammer's job. Spook and his partner would stay in Portland to gather as much information as possible. Hammer and Bill would fly back to Colorado Springs and gather equipment for the teams. Spook gave him a list.

The two young members of the previous team were called. Hammer thought they might want another crack at the top members of the al-Qaeda cell. Arrangements were made and any equipment they needed was obtained through previous sources. Hammer had brought many of the items with him in the duffle bags.

Information was coming in from Portland on a daily basis. Spook and his partner were doing an excellent job continuing the stakeouts on the company building and properties that belonged to Larucci and his son; they kept a log of times, schedules, and habits of the main players. They had no doubts now who the main players were and had positively identified Toni and Eli Larucci.

Early on a Thursday, a little over a week from their last meeting, Spook called and gave them a timeline and the go ahead for a meeting the next day. The other two members, the twins Frank and Jeremy, had been living at Hammer's house and were ready for any action. The six would meet at the Troutdale airport at noon.

Hammer, Bill, and the two brothers boarded Lucky Lucy along with all of their gear and departed Peterson Field for Troutdale, just a short distance east of Portland. They made it easily by noon and were met by Spook and Many. They transferred all of the equipment to one of two large SUVs and headed for a motel. Lucky Lucy was put in a hangar.

When they assembled in Portland, the meeting was all business at first as they discussed the information, timetables, and the method for taking over the buildings. There seemed to be a slight deviation in that not all of the top men were in one place. The company consisted of one two-story building and one warehouse 150 yards away. Larucci senior spent most of his time in the two-story office building. The son was flying his helicopter to Tillamook, on the coast, a little over eighty miles away. Hammer and Bill would handle the son while the others would split, each team taking the business building or warehouse. They actually needed more men, but they agreed that the operation could be completed with a reasonable amount of success with what they had.

The raid would be started when the signal was given with all of the top people confirmed and in sight. The challenge Hammer and Bill faced was to find the bungalow and observe the target until they received a signal from Spook" to move in. The other teams would continue surveillance on the two buildings in Portland. They all would monitor listening devices and would signal each other when to begin, verifying that the major players were in place and then and only then commit to a "go" for the operation. They would not lose this bunch again. All would be in position by four in the afternoon the next day to observe any activity and prepare for the signal. When the signal was given from Spook", the three teams would strike and strike hard, all at once

The men retired to their rooms and cleaned weapons and prepared any other equipment. New batteries were installed for communications and their clothes were made ready. Hammer pulled Jeremy to one side and discussed his plans. He added a few requests of his own. Before going to their rooms, Hammer mentioned the fact that the FBI had discovered the mole in the department and that there could be another. Hammer wanted no doubt or questions about anybody during the operation.

Hammer showed extreme confidence in each member of the team. He had to because there was no one else. They were ready. Bill, on the other hand, had become a little skeptical. He was showing signs of hesitation and a loss of short-term memory. Hammer was concerned, but had no doubts in Bill's ability, assuring the others that everything was as it should be; they both were ready for action.

CHAPTER 22

The morning flight started under a 5,000-foot ceiling with no wind. Hammer and Bill took off from Troutdale and flew south. Twenty miles north of Salem they turned west and dropped down to the valley floor, following the contour of the land to the coast. The Golden Eagle took little time eating up the distance, barely above the tree tops and cruising about 300 miles an hour. Turning north along the coast, Tillamook appeared in a break between two ridges in the distance and they soon landed and taxied to the fuel island. Lucky Lucy was fueled and tied down in a spot that would enable a quick exit. Hammer didn't know the exact odds he and Bill would be facing. Their plan was to do their business and then get back to Portland and the hotel as soon as possible; the other teams might need help.

A rental car was waiting for them and as Hammer finished his tasks, Bill loaded their equipment. Trying out the small handheld GPS and selecting the desired coordinates, the two started their drive through the rich green of the valley floor. They were unable to miss the large silhouette of the old blimp hangar, marked "Museum" on the roof at the southeast end of the airport. Passing the city limits sign on the old coast highway on the south side of the city, they stopped on an old road that overlooked the valley and city. They prepared their equipment, unloading the duffle bags, and dressed for the operation. Traffic on the main road was minimal.

They concealed the fact that they were heavily armed and capable of holding their own. They made their last check of their weapons, communications, and any devices they had.

Hammer pushed a few buttons on the GPS and the south part of the city of Tillamook showed on the screen. He was not sure of the actual location of the bungalow, but had a rural address that would bring them close enough. Hammer also had a space view of the terrain, showing their present location. It indicated that they were close. Air traffic seemed to be at a minimum as the two watched from a bluff overlooking the valley. Daylight was hindered by the overcast sky. The Pacific Ocean was west of where they stood. Through binoculars, they could see Lucky Lucy with her long snout tied down at the airport. She blended in with the rest of the light aircraft. The ocean breeze was typically west-southwesterly at ten knots or more and the area was expecting a storm to move in after midnight.

Hammer pushed the activation button on the GPS to guide them to the bungalow and the two started driving, hoping to find an access road close to the bungalow to park so they would have a better means of retreat if anything went wrong. They were in luck with a gravel road just a short ways before what looked like the driveway to the bungalow.

They parked the car and gathered whatever gear they needed. Giving each other a high five, they were ready to rumble. Bill, always pretending to be John Wayne, made the typical Hollywood wagon master motion with an open hand saying "Tallyho." And then they were off on foot toward what they hoped would be the last of their grief.

Miniature listening devices were small, but efficient, and the twins, positioned with a clear path to the front of the three-story building, listened for familiar voices. The front was mainly surrounded by windows and from their location details were easy to pick up with the small directional mikes and binoculars; the employees spoke about shipments and the typical business talk, moving items to various places up and down the coast. Most of the conversations were in English and were about the business and bits of personal info, but eventually turned toward the movements of arms and explosives. A call from some other company was taken at three thirty and was a conversation about family at first and then changed to explosives being shipped out. Toni also talked to his son and told him that he was not needed for two days. The twins relayed the information to Hammer and Bill on the satellite phone. That was a break for them.

From the GPS and satellite picture, Hammer and Bill quickly found a structure they believed to be the bungalow. They set up their listening stations on the front side, slightly above the structure on the northern slope of neighboring hills, with a clear line of sight. It didn't take long to activate the equipment and identify the sound of voices, one of which was hopefully Eli's. The two men confirmed the presence of two people in the house and they continued scanning while waiting to detect any other voices. They wanted no surprises.

Ten minutes passed and no other voices or visible people were detected in the bungalow. Hammer and Bill made their way through trees and light terrain; they were now within striking distance. Bill identified Eli through his small field binoculars and gave the nod to Hammer.

The three teams were in constant contact with each other. Hammer, waiting for the "go" signal, pressed the ear piece for the satellite phone deeper in to his ear. He was tense. He didn't want to miss the signal. The overcast and the trees made the area seem like twilight. Bill kept visible contact between Eli and his companion using his scope. They still needed to know the exact number of hostiles they would be dealing with. They went with two.

They waited, but not long. In the ear piece of the satellite phone, Hammer was alerted to the other team's activities. The team's updates were coming in more frequently and when everyone was in position and the timing was perfect they again rehearsed the "go" signal three times. Hammer would give Bill an audible and visual signal when to move in.

As they sat, listening and watching the activity in the bungalow, they both could hear loud music and a scream once in a while.

Bill could hear that the man played rough with his girl. The two maintained visual contact and just waited.

At four twenty seven in the afternoon the raids began with "Go! Go! Go!" They both ran, Hammer to the front and Bill to the back porch, both dressed in camo gear and masks. They both had silenced Sig Sauer .40 caliber pistols drawn. They also had compact CAR 15s slung across their back. Hammer eased open the front door about six inches and pulled the pin of a stun grenade, releasing the clip and counting two seconds before rolling it across the living room floor where the music and voices were coming from. He slowly shut the door, covering his ears and eyes with his palms. Even looking in the opposite direction and with his ears covered he could sense a bright flash and hear a deep *rrummppff*.

Almost immediately after the sound, he and Bill went through the doors. They seized the two people in the lightly smoke-filled room by the hair with faces down. The two squirming and wriggling forms were not hard to find, moving in slow motion and in pain on the floor. All of their senses were distorted by the magnitude of the blast and they lay incapacitated with a trickle of blood from ears and noses. Any aggression from either one would be unexpected after the massive trauma to the senses. Hammer, in the living room with a handful of the man's hair, pulled his head back to compare a picture from his vest pocket with the actual face. It was Eli all right.

Hammer pulled several plastic ties from his vest and secured both of Eli's feet and arms behind his back. Eli was now trying to kick and bite and used every swear word in the book. Bill did the same with the other person, a girl in her mid-twenties. When Bill had finished banding her hands and feet and putting a motel pillow cover over her head he said, "Don't move or else." She became rigid at the words and started crying. Bill said, "Take it easy. The effect of the stun grenade will wear off."

Eli was more vocal in his high-pitched voice, asking for mercy and at the same time telling everyone he would kill them all. He tried to wriggle free, only succeeding in making his bonds tighter and being gagged. He too now had a pillow case over his head. He made it difficult, twisting and spinning like a dogfish just pulled into a boat. He demanded to be set free and complained about the intrusion to his house, all through the gag in his mouth. When the two were secure, Hammer and Bill searched the entire bungalow.

A small safe, partially opened, and a leather attaché case full of papers and money were found. There were several weapons and pieces of equipment Hammer tossed in one of two empty duffle bags. Hammer grabbed a set of keys on the counter. Finishing the search, Hammer went to the front room and sat down beside Eli. Bill went for the car. Hammer didn't know whether he was going to put a couple of rounds in Eli's head or just bust him up. Bill had the same look when he came through the front door after getting the car. The two thought better and gathered all of the documents in bags, carrying them to the car along with another large duffle bag. They carried the two men, tied and gagged and resisting, to the car, tossing them in to the backseat.

Bill went back in to the bungalow and searched one more time for any hidden stashes of information. He then did his magic by setting several thermal charges, activating switches on them just before exiting the front door.

He jumped into the passenger seat and at a hundred yards down the road Hammer stopped. Bill got out and reached into his vest pocket, retrieving a small remote with a short antenna. He raised the guard covering a small switch and extended the antenna to full length. He then pressed the switch, sending a signal to the bungalow and triggering the thermal charges. Since Eli had been yelling and swearing the whole time, Bill slid in the backseat next to him. The girl just sat, but Eli persisted on making a fuss. Bill smacked him in the face with the back of his fist. A slight crack was heard and a little blood oozed down and appeared on the white pillow case. "A broken nose might settle this guy down," Bill said.

At first there was not much effect, but once fueled, the high-heat devices did their job and as the car drove away, Hammer could see the bungalow fully engulfed in flames in the rearview mirror.

Hammer took a different route going back than he did coming. He set coordinates in the GPS and followed the arrow and the road displayed on the small screen.

After fifteen minutes they started crossing a bridge spanning part of a four-mile long lake surrounded by dense, tall Douglas firs. Hammer slowed the car and came to a stop in the middle of the bridge crossing a smaller inlet. There was no traffic or people in the area. Both Hammer and Bill got out and Hammer grabbed Eli, dragging him to the rail. Till now, hardly a word had been said by Hammer or Bill. Hammer wanted to take Eli out ten miles to sea and dump him from the plane, but couldn't. There was no way to open a door to let him out of Lucky Lucy. Bill wanted to just shoot them both. The final decision was to attach weights to the body of Eli and toss him in the water.

As the two began to hoist Eli over the side, his feet were almost wet when Hammer called a halt and pulled him back up. He said, "Not so fast. This is for all of the victims you killed and the lives you ruined. This is also for Francis." Hammer took his Sig out and put a round in each of Eli's knees, shattering the bone and splattering tissue over a six-foot area on the bridge. Eli was screaming through the gag in his mouth as Bill made sure the weights were firm on Eli's feet and legs, giving him a few extra pulls on the knees. He wrote on one weight, "This one's for Francis." That wouldn't get even, but it would cause enough pain to help ease Hammer's a little.

Hammer and Bill Picked up the terrorist's squirming and bleeding body and slipped Eli into the greenish deep water. Still screaming in pain and fear through the gag in his mouth, the only sounds that remained as the water covered his head, slowly slipping under the surface, was the sound of bubbles as he sunk to the depths of 150 feet below. The bubbles lasted only seconds. All traces of Eli were now gone except the splattered blood, which would be washed away by the coming storm.

Hammer and Bill were long gone by the time the last bubble reached the surface. The body would decompose before it was found, if ever.

Hammer reset the GPS to guide them back to the airport. It was almost total dark by the time they got there and they drove right to the plane.

Hammer prepared Lucky Lucy for flight while Bill loaded all of the equipment and their passenger. Hammer noticed a dark helicopter sitting a hundred yards away so he drove over to it, taking out the keys he had found at the bungalow and trying them. Sure enough, they fit. He locked it back up and drove back to Lucky Lucy where he told Bill the keys fit. They both smiled. Soon the plane was airborne and they were on their way back to Troutdale. Hammer retraced their course through the hills and up the valley, the same way they had come.

After landing Bill left for the car and Hammer tied the plane down. They both loaded the equipment and their now motionless bundle into the back of the car. The three headed for Lloyd Center where they pulled into an area well away from cameras and in the darker part of the parking lot. They took the girl out and cut the plastic ties on her wrists and ankles. Bill told her not to move for five minutes. He also said, "You are a very lucky young lady tonight. The man you were with was a terrorist and a killer. He has killed many your age. Most of his victims are buried at sea." She started to cry.

The girl heard the car leave and she waited for a few minutes to move. She was still in shock from the concussion grenade and flight when she removed the pillow case. She then freed her hands and feet and forced herself to stand. She found two envelopes that had fallen to the ground when she stood. She picked them both up and opened the smaller one. The envelope contained $5,000 and a note that read, "Make better choices." She turned and walked toward the lights, knowing she was lucky to be alive.

Hammer and Bill arrived at the hotel, parking the car and carrying the equipment to their room. They met with the others in Spook's room. Their mood was one of relief and exhaustion. They all were full of excitement and celebration because their operation was successful and they were all alive. Each team began to tell its stories and, as usual, some parts were true and some were not.

Both of the other teams were not as sympathetic as Hammer and Bill. The twins went into the building that housed the business office when all but the main objective had gone. Only two security guards were left along with the senior Larucci and one of his henchmen.

One of the twins used a small electronic device to gain entrance through the side door and systematically the twins swept the entire building, eliminating all of the occupants with silenced .40 caliber shots to the head.

They found the senior Larucci in his office with his vault open, a lucky sight to both Franky and Jeremy who immediately emptied the contents, placing the old man inside with a couple of .40 cals in his temple. Another henchman was left where he fell from another .40 cal. They verified the body of Tony Larucci with pictures. Activating the arm switch on a thermal device, they placed the body and the device in the safe and shut the door. They placed more devices in strategic places and armed them while securing the duffle bags filled with the items from the safe and headed down to the car. Less than a block away they stopped and activated a small remote. Nothing dramatic happened like explosions or fireballs, but the two of them knew that the contents of the safe were nothing but cinder and the office building was all but destroyed. They left the building for the motel.

Spook and his partner at the warehouse really did not expect to find much, but Spook took care of two guards while his partner found another to dispose of. The warehouse itself was filled with all sorts of machinery and parts. Most were for boats and ships. It was only by dumbfound luck and previous experience with other Larucci properties that they happened to catch the last man closing a hidden door to a stairway leading into a large warehouse basement filled with crates and boxes and a small office space to one side. It appeared that they had found the last of the main networking centers for the west coast and what Spook had been looking for all this time. Spook climbed back up the stairs and out a nearby door. He made a call while outside and then headed back in to see just what exactly they had stumbled upon. They took pictures of all of the guards, the equipment, and the warehouse.

The two teams, Spook's and the twins, met back at the hotel after disposing of their clothes. The clothes were dumped and the used equipment was disassembled and thrown in the Columbia River. They patiently waited for the last two, still not back from

Tillamook. It wasn't long before Hammer and Bill got to the motel. They had gotten rid of their equipment from the sky. A barrel of a pistol was easier to drop than a body. There would be no trace of the pistols. Bill told the group about their operation and what they found. He only left out a few things. Hammer just sat in peace.

Everyone had questions. Hammer went first with his and Bill's success and what they had found. They had dropped the girl in Portland on the way back along with giving her a file with news clippings of six missing girls and GPS coordinates found in the attaché. The team asked about Eli's dump site. All that Hammer said was, "There would be no dust to dust for his funeral." Neither Hammer nor Bill would ever divulge the location of Eli's body.

Next, Spook let everyone know about what they had found at the warehouse. He casually stated, "Shipping manifests and lots of equipment was about it." And then he lied, "Only a minimum of arms." The twins told about clearing the building and that the safe was just being closed when they had found Larucci. After they shot him and they checked the safe, they found only records for payroll and taxes. The papers that were found in the warehouse must have been Larucci's main stash. At least that was the assumption of the twins. As ordered, they lied too.

The monster had been slain, the head cut off and the chain of information to al-Qaeda outside the United States broken.

It was getting late and the team members didn't feel like anything but sleep. Spook and his partner dismissed themselves, with the twins leaving for their motel and Hammer and Bill to theirs. When in their room, Bill was hungry so he ordered room service. Hammer just lay on the bed in subtle alert. Bill wondered what he was up to and wasn't surprised when he heard a knock on the door. Hammer got up and answered it. It was one of the twins and he handed Hammer a large duffle bag. The twin said good night and that was the end of the waiting for Hammer. He picked up the phone and ordered a New York steak medium-rare and a salad.

The next morning Hammer made a call to his family. His only words were to Sandy: "We can go home now." After hanging up he called a friend at the airport at Troutdale, letting him know where a key was hidden. Hammer had made arrangements for a friend to fly the helicopter from Tillamook to Troutdale and store it in a hangar.

The whole group met for a late breakfast in the hotel restaurant. Hammer gave everyone envelopes with large amounts of money to cover any inconvenience and whatever equipment they used. Also, travel vouchers were handed out. Private cell numbers were exchanged in the event that any other jobs might come up. Both Hammer and Bill said emphatically, "No more for us!" The men said their goodbyes and left. Hammer and Bill headed for the airport and Lucky Lucy. They would be back in Colorado Springs in the early evening.

The trip was made like all others from the coast to the mid-Colorado town. Any threat having been eliminated, they still had a habit of not travelling in a straight line. The law was not what they wanted to deal with and some of the things the men had done in the past day were certainly not likely to be looked on by the local constables as legal, especially dumping bodies and burning buildings. They stayed as low as they dared over the Columbia River gorge, keeping above cables and veering off toward Rock Springs for fuel. They flew mostly direct this time and not to the opposite direction they were intending to fly. Their transponder was off. It might have taken more fuel and time, but this route left a cold trail. From Rock Springs Lucky Lucy flew at a low level to the high rim of the Rockies above the Boulder area, once again dropping down to the valley floor and skirting the mountain bases and landing at Peterson Field. At no time did Hammer ever speak on the radio on his trip back, except to Peterson tower. He wanted no trail to this trip and his airplane.

The two guided the airplane into the hangar as the tug chugged away, pushing the larger airplane. It was evening and the airfield had closed down. By this time and flying so much with Hammer, Bill had now been able to at least steer the plane, allowing Hammer to catch up on a few hours of sleep on the way back. Both were dead-tired, but with a new attitude. They shut the hangar door, having loaded the equipment and the large duffle bag into the van.

The girls were excited to see them both and so were the four dogs. The two travelers probably smelled ripe to interest the dogs. Sandy wanted to hear about the operation and the girls wanted to go out for dinner, but both Hammer and Bill were mostly interested in a shower and some shut-eye. It was hard for the girls to contain themselves knowing that there were no more threats lurking as they locked the doors of their Woodland Park home, surrounded by the clear star-filled skies of Colorado. They could all view the moon illuminating the bright silhouette of Pike's Peak in the distance. This was a picture-perfect conclusion for a brutal last few days for both Hammer and Bill.

About 10:00 A.M. Hammer was awakened by a phone call from Spook. He wanted to meet at the Antler Plaza Hotel the next afternoon and Hammer agreed. How did Spook know where they were? Hammer no longer wondered about the comments the twins had made about Spook. Contrary to what Hammer believed, Spook maintained his unpredictability.

The morning came and the two warriors had gotten some sleep. Sandy had wanted to wake them, but thought better of the idea. Pancakes and coffee were served and eventually they got around to the canvas containers. The hard part was the lock, but a pair of bolt cutters solved the problem.

The contents immediately spewed on the floor. Nothing surprising was evident as the typical files and cash were revealed. Not showing any excitement, Hammer concentrated on what Spook wanted. The three began counting and eventually came up with a total.

Hammer and Bill were apprehensive about the meeting and wondered just what Spook was up to. Hammer took no chances so with Bill and his drawn Sig a few steps behind him, proceeded to the meeting place. Hammer knocked on the door and was greeted by Spook. There were others in the room besides Spook. Hammer moved forward, eyeing the situation, and then gave Bill the sign to come ahead. Bill knew something was up so he slowly moved forward with his Sig in the flap of his coat, making one last scan in the hallway and then the room area, staying close with his back to the wall.

Spook introduced the men in the room. "I would like to introduce you to deputy director Samuel Speirs of the Central Intelligence Agency, and Thomas Reins and Kirk Harvey, bureau chiefs of his unit, my bosses." Somehow Hammer wasn't surprised. He shook hands, examined their identification badges and cards and sat on the sofa. Spook had been an active CIA undercover operative all this time, assigned to find and report on the al-Qaeda factor on the west coast and the contacts they used in the eastern countries sponsoring the activities. They had co-operation and clearance from the FBI for the deep cover, since the FBI was concerned about a possible mole in the unit. . Hammer whispered in Bill's ear, "No wonder it was so easy to get guns and equipment."

The deputy director's first statement was, "You two have been busy." Hammer and Bill looked at each other and smiled. They were then asked to keep any of the following discussion and information exchanged in the room confidential. This meeting had been deemed classified and therefore, "top secret." Again, Hammer looked at Bill and they both smiled. Samuel came right to the point, making it clear that they wanted all of the information Hammer and Bill had, including what the twins had gathered and all of the money.

Hammer was not one to buckle to commands at this time in his life and neither was Bill. They had worked too hard and sacrificed too much for any demands thrown at them. Hammer looked at Bill and then at Spook and said, "We will give you some of what you asked for, except that some of the money was spent on the operations and replacing damaged property." They would give the CIA the files of information and half of the money. The other half would be used for their relocation. Hammer made it known that there was no other way to divide the money.

The three men discussed the terms and the director said, "We want all of the money."

Hammer replied, "I have an item that could be of better use than the money." He then explained about the helicopter he had stored in a hangar.

The deputy director looked at the other two men and then at Hammer and nodded. Hammer took out his cell phone and placed a call. In one minute, there was a knock on the door and Sandy was there with a large case and two boxes of documents. Hammer said, "The only reason we wanted to find these documents was to see if they had any more information on my family or on Bill."

The director asked, "Did they?"

"Nope," Hammer replied. And then he added, "One more thing."

Spook nodded. "Go ahead."

"I would like a total tax amnesty for any money and holdings Bill or I currently have. The money is mine to use and give for any reason."

The deputy director said, "That is a stiff request. Do you have any more helicopters?"

Hammer chuckled and said, "No, but I do have other things that I will keep for awhile."

The deputy director was not particularly happy with that statement, but realized that Hammer's family had been through enough hardship. So had Bill and his health was an issue. The director said with tension, "Okay."

Hammer and Bill didn't particularly enjoy being near these CIA types and so they excused themselves, along with Sandy. Before they had a chance to leave the deputy director said, "You remember that none of this conversation and information about the operations can ever be talked about?"

Hammer and Bill both nodded, not particularly liking the subtle threat. The director looked at Sandy and she too nodded. He continued by saying, "If that's acceptable and you all agree, *representing* the United States Government and the CIA, I would like to thank you for a dangerous job well done."

Hammer and Bill were humbled and shook hands with all of the men. Just before their departure, Hammer pulled Spook to one side and spoke to him for a few minutes. Then they shook hands and said their goodbyes. As Hammer, Bill and Sandy got into their car Bill looked at Hammer and said, "At least we don't have to worry about hauling that junk in the duffle bag around anymore." Bill seemed to be his old self with humor and a quick step. They all laughed and headed back to the house.

When they arrived home, Hammer called a meeting of the family and together they all sat around the dining room table. Talking about what their plans were and what the girls might think, all of their opinions were shared. Sandy said that she missed Alaska and wanted to go back to continue her job if it was still available. Bill, on the other hand, loved the weather in the Springs area. He would keep the house they were in. It was paid for by the terrorists and set up like he wanted, so he was quite happy. Hammer loved Colorado Springs and the mountains. After all, this was where he had been born. He also loved Alaska and the rugged, simple life. He was not going to stop flying, which was his true love. The weather was better by far in Colorado. However, he thought of the girls. He asked both of them for their wishes. After all, they could always visit Bill and Bill could always visit them. For the first time in a long while, the girls had a say and the family wasn't held hostage and in pursuit.

Jackie liked the Springs area and liked Alaska too. She was just glad not to be on the run and not hiding anymore. She would go wherever everyone else decided. Amanda, on the other hand, was attached to Sandy. She would go wherever Sandy went. The majority vote was in and the family decided where they wanted to live. Unanimously, it was apparent that a move back to the very place it all started was the choice. Alaska was in their blood.

Hammer had enough money that he surely did not have to work. He expressed his concern about a new business, which was always his intent, as long as it had to do with flying. He would open a new service or help Katie with the old one. Hammer was somewhat leery of the Dillingham area because of possible lingering al-Qaeda operatives, but Bill reassured him that all of the dossiers passed to the CIA told of no more operatives in the area and that the family would be safe. Hammer muttered under his breath, "Famous last words."

The family members made their final arrangements and decided on a specific date to fly back to Alaska. Sandy was not too surprised to hear her last job had been taken, but there was an opening in Homer, which she accepted. That changed some of Hammer's plans, but, after a few calls to Anchorage and Homer, he decided to open a service out of Homer and work together with Katie as a partnership in Dillingham.

The day had come to leave and the four of them, plus two dogs, boarded a commercial flight first class from Peterson to Denver and then on to Anchorage. They left Bill and James at the terminal looking sad to see them go. James had washed and cleaned Lucky Lucy inside and out, assuming they were going to fly her. The hangar was made immaculate. As Bill and James locked the hangar with Lucky Lucy tucked inside and were about to head for an early lunch, they were greeted by an army officer who asked if they would kindly join the commanding officer in the headquarters building at Fort Carson. Bill and James had no idea what was going on but they followed the lieutenant to an olive-drab car and were taken to a building at the fort. Getting out of the car, the officer led them to the brick headquarters building and then to a larger room half-filled with people. James knew none of them except for his daughter. He was overjoyed to see her and gave her a huge hug.

Spook and Hammer had talked to the military unit that investigated servicemen and women deserving medals of valor and gave them James' name. A file was found in the New Orleans office of military personnel, a box on some obscure shelf in the back of some old warehouse. The overlooked file described the many heroic deeds that James had accomplished. One told how he helped save a downed pilot and officer from being overrun by the North Vietnamese.

On that special day, the commanding officer in charge of Fort Carson, the same officer James had saved, awarded the Silver Star to James. James and his daughter, looking on from in front of the crowd of distinguished guests, would never have to worry about living expenses again, including living in that small house on the outskirts of Colorado Springs. James was given a well-deserved position with the army to help recruit service members. Two months later, he was called to Washington, DC and presented the nation's highest award, the Congressional Medal of Honor, given by the president himself. From then on, James would start a tour of the United States and other countries as a representative of the armed services.

The commander of the Air force Academy also made sure that James had season tickets every year to football games. He knew James loved the game and that he had saved a downed air force pilot during his time in 'nam.

After the ceremony and back at the hangar, Bill handed James an envelope just before leaving for home and his dogs. James sat on the steps of the hangar and opened the envelope. Inside were two sets of keys and a note. The note was from Hammer and said, "We are all very proud to know you and have you as our friend. Come visit sometime." It was signed, "Wayne Carpenter and family plus Bill." The tag on the first set of keys said "Gator" and the other set was marked "Hangar 46 South." Along with the keys was an airplane title release and a signed bill of sale for the hangar in James' name. Tucked away at the bottom was also a prepaid credit card. A statement of accounts indicated a balance of $100,000. James was unsure of the first set of keys so he went back into the hangar and turned on the lights. Below the pilot window of the Golden Eagle, instead of "Lucky Lucy" was the name "Gator," with a smiling alligator face below. It was almost too much for James as he walked to the door, shutting off the lights and closing it behind him. He again sat on the steps to the hangar door and started to tear.

CHAPTER 23

Hammer had grown attached to the larger twin-engine airplanes and as soon as possible he purchased a Piper Chieftain. This plane would be a complement to the two 336s and could carry more freight and passengers. He had been communicating with Katie and had helped her with problem areas of her company. Now that he was back he could help with the maintenance and paperwork associated with running her air taxi business. He certainly did not want to get in Katie's way, just help and be involved with the flying.

The family settled in again. Hammer had just signed papers for his own air taxi service and was set up with a nice hangar at the Homer airport. The new Chieftain was a great airplane for the Alaska area and tough as nails. It could carry a sizable load of about 1,300 pounds with just Hammer onboard and full fuel. The girls quickly named it "Brutus" for being fatter and larger than the 421. Hammer eventually had the plane painted, refurbished, and equipped with new avionics.

The amount of flying they did the first six months brought the engine time up to a need for overhaul and a couple of new 350 horsepower turbocharged Continental engines were installed. Hammer loved the characteristics of the counter-rotating props. Katie would call if she needed a larger airplane for a trip and he made as many trips to Dillingham as he could to help with her airplane maintenance. Sandy thought there was some kind of an attachment growing.

Sandy was back doing what she loved: working in the field and watching over the native wildlife. She too had an interest in one particular of the opposite sex, a local business owner she had met several years before. She still spent time with the family, but the girls were busy with school activities and it seemed that she was less and less in demand.

Jackie, a junior now, was on the volleyball team and had a boyfriend Hammer was not really fond of. He tried not to be the worrisome parent and hoped all would turn out. However, he would always make the comment to Jackie, "Anyone who wore his pants that low had something wrong with him." Hammer hoped it was a passing fancy. Her grades had slipped and he always had to remind her that if she wanted to go to college, the grades had better improve. Her usual reply was the typical, "Ah, Dad."

Amanda, the "sparkplug" of the family, still patterned herself after Sandy. She had passed her third-degree black belt test in tae kwon do and was working on her fourth degree. She entered all of the local and Anchorage tournaments, usually taking top honors. She had understood what school was all about at an early age and was an A student.

The lodge at Iliamna was always busy and the owners had to hire more staff to help run the business. Guides had been hired and there was air service most every day. One of the 336s was used exclusively for the lodge service. Hammer and Katie were thinking of getting a 206 for this, but they hadn't made arrangements yet. Katie had hired a pilot just for that route.

One afternoon of sun, Hammer was just sitting down for lunch at home when the phone rang. He answered to the sound of Spook's voice. Spook was in Homer and wanted to meet. Hammer agreed, thinking, "They sure keep track of me."

The meeting was over cups of coffee at the airport café. The CIA was extremely impressed with Hammer and Bill and the teams they had assembled. Hammer asked, "Have you found any documents identifying me and my family?"

Spook shook his head.

Spook explained he was interested in having Hammer and Bill work for the company and made them a serious offer. They both knew the region and with Hammer's leadership skills, he would be a perfect match for some of their operations. But Hammer's answer was an emphatic "Nope!", at least not at this time. Hammer said he couldn't speak for Bill and told him Bill's phone number.

Spook stood and shook hands, giving Hammer a business card at the same time. Hammer said, "See ya' later," and watched as Spook walked out to a waiting Saberliner. Spook climbed up the few stairs and passed through the open door of the plane. Hammer looked down at the card that read, "Dennis A. Maxwell, assistant deputy director, western division, CIA, Denver, Colorado." Hammer thought, "Well Mr. Maxwell, I hope we never meet again."

Two weeks had passed since Bill called Alaska. He wasn't as lonely as he had been since Hammer and the girls left. He loved the scenery and climate of Woodland Park but was still missing a part of his past life, having teenage girls in the house always presenting new situations to deal with. The aspen trees, along with the green of the other deciduous trees and evergreens, were breathtaking from the view of the front porch. Without Hammer and the kids, the place was definitely empty. He had the dogs, but it wasn't the same.

He had been getting more and more headaches for the last few months, but really had no idea that the cause was anything other than stress. He went to the doctor on Hammer's request and had a scan done. Only recently had he heard back to make an appointment as soon as possible for the results.

To stay busy, it didn't take Bill long to purchase a struggling restaurant and change the name to "Willy's Way," a burger and chili parlor near the fort. It became so busy and popular in Colorado Springs that he had to open another on the north end of town for the "Zoomies."(Air Force cadets)

When Bill met with the doctor, the message was brief and clear. The prognosis was not good. The damage to his brain showed large spots of tissue damage and scarring that was irreparable. The doctor gave him months to live. There was some medication, but only temporary. Bill didn't take it. He kept this to himself. He didn't want to burden others and he would take care of his affairs by himself. His thoughts were that those Larucci thugs had done a better job than he or any one had anticipated and finally had gotten in the last word.

One day, almost a year after the Portland adventure, Hammer received a call from James in Colorado Springs. Evidently Bill had just come home from one of his restaurants and gotten a glass of iced tea. He had gone to the front porch for some rest and time with the dogs. The weather was beautiful and he loved to just look at Pike's Peak with its array of colors. He fell asleep and never woke up. There was a long pause at the end of the line. Hammer was in shock. He felt like he had failed his friend. Hammer knew there was something wrong with Bill and he hadn't done enough to help his best friend. He would now have to live with that.

Hammer, Sandy and the girls made arrangements to fly to Colorado Springs the following week. James met them upon arrival and gave Hammer a note from Bill. Hammer tucked the envelope in his pocket to read at a time he was alone.

James took Hammer and his family to the house and then to the service that had been planned for the small group. Spook had flown in just after Hammer and joined the family. The service was short on Bill's request and then the body was taken by the military honor guard and placed on a plane to Washington, DC. Sandy and the kids took Bill's dogs and headed back to Alaska, while Hammer escorted the coffin. As usual, Spook disappeared.

Bill received full honors at Arlington National Cemetery. As the final sound of taps was heard, Hammer removed the note from his pocket and read it.

Hammer, if you are reading this there is only one reason, the doctors were right. Larucci's men were good at what they did, but never broke me. It's been a pleasure these last year's flying all over the country with you and there is no one I would have rather had as a friend than you. My thoughts will always be with you and the family. Take care of the dogs, everything else should be good.

Tallyho,
Bill

During the time Mark Glenrose spent as the unit expert in the field and as team leader for the FBI's terrorism department in Anchorage, he established guidelines that were used to organize data and expedite quick, immediate deployment for operations involving al-Qaeda cells and other terrorist factions. Structured operations and the resultant information gained by his team's actions proved his worth as a top agent and leader. Descriptions of his first and only case in the state, leading to the disclosure of many al-Qaeda top operatives and their activities, were submitted to the main office and later used as examples for bureau training. These techniques and his story of how they were established are brought forth from the case of the "Top Secret" file known as "The Larucci Files."

POST SCRIPT
EIGHT MONTHS LATER

This was the second fisherman that Hammer had to pick up from Nikolski, a small town on the northwest side of Umnak Island, part of the Fox Islands and the Aleutian chain, in the last three months. Having been in Dutch Harbor for the night after dropping off four of the Aleutian Housing Administration members, he received a call from state troopers asking if he could bring the fisherman back to Kenai. He had an empty plane and was in the mood so he volunteered.

Starting out to Nikolski early the next morning, he arrived and landed on the 3,500-foot gravel strip, taxiing to the turn around on the north side. The carcass of the old Reeve DC-3 was still there, corroding and full of holes. He walked to the little store and post office combination where one of the natives offered him a cup of coffee while another went for the fisherman. After a ten-minute wait and a conversation with the postmaster about what was happening up north, the fisherman arrived and he and Hammer headed for the plane. Hammer started up the engines and taxied the plane for takeoff, doing a quick mag check on the way and setting his compass. They were airborne in no time and headed straight for Cold Bay and then King Salmon.

Hammer casually questioned the fisherman who was riding in the right front seat and found that he had been stranded on a spit off Samalga Island near the western tip of Umnak Island. He had been aboard the Mary Kay, a seventy-foot fishing boat that was just emptying the last net of fish into its hold. Unknown to them, four men in an inflatable boat came aboard from the bow of the ship. They were all dressed in black and all had automatic weapons. They shot the captain right off and proceeded to sail to the spit. He had no idea at first where their exact location was, but when he saw the island he knew.

The rest of the crew was given a choice of swimming to the spit or being crab food. While the others were deciding, he made a leap over the side and was hidden between waves and turbulent water, having had to swim under the surface as far as possible to distance himself from the ship. Despite their words, some rifles were fired at him with fortunately none of the bullets hitting the target. The water was extremely cold, but he was the only one not shot and dumped overboard. They must have been in a hurry because they sailed off without looking for him.

He barely made the one hundred yards to the spit, crawling up under some beach debris and hiding out of the wind under sea weed and beach clutter; his body regained vital temperature. He set a beach fire with his cigarette lighter and was just beginning to stoke it with more wood when he saw a smaller fishing boat. With apprehension, the approaching boat sent their small tender to fetch him from the small body of land. In that area or any other, fishing boats sometime let crew members off on land if they become a problem. The Mary Kay, minus the crew, had not been seen since.

No trace is what Doug, the leader of the boarding party wanted. His teams of worldwide mixed ex-military personnel, displeased with what the world was all about, were anxious to seize and take over more and more boats. The teams would unload the precious cargo to a rogue processor and sail them empty to Herbert Island where they were scrapped and sold for parts, a large and profitable industry around the world.

Hammer was interested to hear the fisherman's story because it was similar to one another fisherman's experience from a few months ago. The two were lucky to be alive and survive these pirates. Hammer thought about where they might be holed up, but a little voice inside his head warned him about the last time he decided to go gung-ho. Besides, the trail was already cold.

Hammer dropped the fisherman off in Kenai and then headed home to Homer. He landed and taxied over to the pumps for fuel. He then taxied to his hangar and put the Chieftain inside. It took him very little time to get back to the house and to his study where he pulled out a series of maps. The maps would show him the area that the fisherman was talking about and possible hiding places for a boat. He found the location quickly. The challenge was in his head and he would investigate further. Without Bill, he wondered if he could manage such a task.

After a short daydream, he eagerly sat in front of his computer and pressed the power button.